ALWAYS THE LYON TAMER

The Lyon's Den Connected World

Emily E K Murdoch

ARE YOU SIGNED UP FOR DRAGONBLADE'S BLOG?

You'll get the latest news and information on exclusive giveaways, exclusive excerpts, coming releases, sales, free books, cover reveals and more.

Check out our complete list of authors, too!

No spam, no junk. That's a promise!

Sign Up Here

www.dragonbladepublishing.com

Dearest Reader;

Thank you for your support of a small press. At Dragonblade Publishing, we strive to bring you the highest quality Historical Romance from the some of the best authors in the business. Without your support, there is no 'us', so we sincerely hope you adore these stories and find some new favorite authors along the way.

Happy Reading!

CEO, Dragonblade Publishing

Additional Dragonblade books by Author Emily E K Murdoch

Never The Bride Series
Always the Bridesmaid (Book 1)
Always the Chaperone (Book 2)
Always the Courtesan (Book 3)
Always the Best Friend (Book 4)
Always the Wallflower (Book 5)
Always the Bluestocking (Book 6)
Always the Rival (Book 7)
Always the Matchmaker (Book 8)
Always the Widow (Book 9)
Always the Rebel (Book 10)

The Lyon's Den Connected World
Always the Lyon Tamer

Other Lyon's Den Books
Into the Lyon's Den by Jade Lee
The Scandalous Lyon by Maggi Andersen
Fed to the Lyon by Mary Lancaster
The Lyon's Lady Love by Alexa Aston
The Lyon's Laird by Hildie McQueen
The Lyon Sleeps Tonight by Elizabeth Ellen Carter
A Lyon in Her Bed by Amanda Mariel
Fall of the Lyon by Chasity Bowlin
Lyon's Prey by Anna St. Claire
Loved by the Lyon by Collette Cameron
The Lyon's Den in Winter by Whitney Blake
Kiss of the Lyon by Meara Platt

CHAPTER ONE

MISS REBECCA DARBY swallowed down all her fears, the questions she knew were impertinent, the desire to run, and the panic she knew would overwhelm her if it took hold.

This was madness. How on earth had she managed to get to this position?

Her mother had always said, *dire times called for desperate measures.* As she looked around the Ladies Parlor in the Lyon's Den, Rebecca's smile flickered.

She never thought she would come here—one of the most infamous gentlemen's clubs in London, known for its…well, *debauchery.* Even the word made Rebecca shake.

Rebecca reached into her reticule and pulled out the last letter John Lennox, Marquess of Gloucester, had sent her.

Miss Darby,

I am in receipt of your letter and wish to express my disappointment that I will not be attending Almack's this week and will, therefore, sadly miss you. I am also unlikely to be attending any card parties or balls in London for the rest of the Season.

Yours faithfully,
Gloucester

Rebecca shivered, though the fire in the grate was roaring as was expected on a fresh February evening. It was the coldness of the letter which chilled her blood.

After everything they had shared together—the opera, the carriage rides, the murmured conversations no one else had heard…

She brushed away an angry tear while she waited for the proprietress of the Lyon's Den to meet her as per their appointment. No, she would not shed tears over John Lennox, not yet. Not until she had explored all options.

How was it possible to love a man who hurt you so badly?

A woman wearing a gentleman's breeches, waistcoat, and jacket walked into the room and looked around.

Rebecca stared. Even her good manners could not prevent her; *seeing a woman so wildly dressed, it was unheard of!*

The woman smiled. "Waiting for Mrs. Dove-Lyon?"

Rebecca nodded. Words did not seem sufficient.

The woman's smile broadened. "Aren't we all?"

The door closed behind her before Rebecca could even think of speaking, and she let out a long breath. One of the ladies the Lyon Den employed. This was a world apart from polite society, where a lady in breeches like poor Miss Sophia Worsley last autumn was humiliated, not praised until she became a countess.

The women here were different. They had power in a way Rebecca had never known, never believed possible. They made their own choices—whereas she was forced to live by society's rules.

Was it only a few years ago that they were at the opera? She and John, his brother William, and the woman who would eventually become William's bride?

"My, what a wonderful place! And to think, though my father and I have been in Bath a month, we have not been here! It does not seem quite right that we should come all this way for the Season and not even try some of its delights," Rebecca had said, attempting to demonstrate her worldliness.

And the Duke of Mercia—for that was William's full title, of course—had laughed, and so had Charlotte, and John had hidden his face.

And she had blushed with the shame of it but after that...

A carriage ride where John had stolen kisses. Rebecca's cheeks flushed at the very memory. She should not have let him.

And now he no longer wished to see her, and she had come to the Lyon's Den to...

What?

You cannot think to go through with this, a voice whispered in her ear. *You must be a fool to think you could tame the Lion of the Lennoxes.*

Rebecca rose to her feet. No one but that one lady had seen her here. She could slip through the door and—

"Going somewhere?"

Rebecca jumped. She had not noticed the woman come in, and Mrs. Dove-Lyon was smiling, as though she knew precisely what her guest had been considering.

Curtseying, Rebecca rose to see the proprietress of the Lyon's Den laughing.

"You ladies of society are all the same, stuck to your rules," she said genially. "Come, sit. You will always wonder if you do not hear what I have to say."

Mrs. Dove-Lyon indicated the chair Rebecca had just vacated, but she hesitated.

Was she brave enough to see this through? Did she have the lion tamer's spirit to force John to see her for who she truly was, after he had courted her for so long?

Slowly, she lowered herself into the seat. It did not hurt to hear Mrs. Dove-Lyon's thoughts, after all. *It was just a conversation.*

Mrs. Dove-Lyon nodded as she sat opposite. "You never thought you would be here, did you?"

"No," Rebecca replied honestly, and then, nerves overwhelming her, "Not that I mean any offense, you understand, Mrs. Dove-Lyon, it is just the Lyon's Den is the province of gentlemen. It is most wild of me even to consider being here. My father has no comprehension I am here. He believes me to be spending some time with a friend of mine who is recently in London after being abroad for—"

"Calm yourself, Miss Darby," Mrs. Dove-Lyon said gently, raising a hand to stop the flow of words pouring over her. "I am not offended. You are not the first lady to come here with problems with a gentleman, and you will certainly not be the last."

Rebecca nodded, twisting her hands in her lap. *How did one go about this, then?* All she had heard through the rumor mill was that for a price—and it was a rather hefty price, too—Mrs. Dove-Lyon could…well.

Solve gentlemen problems.

"Now, Miss Darby, you have come with a certain gentleman in mind, I think," said Mrs. Dove-Lyon delicately.

Rebecca took a deep breath and felt her cheeks pink at the very thought of sharing such personal details of her life. *Of her love.*

"My mother died years ago, and my father is very elderly, and I have no siblings to support me or to make him see reason. So, I thought if I came to you, you could—"

"First things first," the woman said emphatically. "Him?"

The fire threw up a spark, and Rebecca glanced over at it, a welcome relief from the penetrating stare of the owner of the Lyon's Den.

This was it. Once she said his name, it would be out in the world for all the gossips to chatter about.

If they were not already talking about her already.

Rebecca swallowed. She had been raised to be a gentlewoman. No great name, nor wealth, but enough respectability to attend the Season as part of the *ton* every year.

But now she was leaving all that behind. The Lyon's Den was no small matter. Once she was a part of its world, it would not matter how good the rest of her life was.

There would be no going back.

John's laughing smile rose in her memory, and she smiled sadly at the recollection. He was hers; she knew it. She knew they belonged together like she knew the night would follow day. Why was that so impossible for him to see?

Mrs. Dove-Lyon was watching her carefully, and Rebecca knew she had to speak. The words had to come out. Besides, Mrs. Dove-Lyon was surely the height of discretion. One could not manage her establishment without the ability to keep one's mouth shut.

"John Lennox, the Marquess of Gloucester," she whispered. "Brother to the Duke of Mercia."

Mrs. Dove-Lyon did not say a word.

Emboldened, Rebecca continued, "It was over two years ago now when he first invited me to the opera—well, it was the duke that did that, but at once I could see 'twas a ruse, for the two of us—John and I went on a carriage ride just a day later. Walks in the park, dancing at Almack's, conversations during which we...I..."

Her voice trailed away. *How did one encapsulate the courting of over a year in a few words?*

"He was everything I wanted, but more than that, he was someone I loved," she said softly. "But then...nothing. I-I wrote to Lady Charlotte, before and after she married the duke, John's brother. She could not help me. And so I wrote to him."

Mrs. Dove-Lyon's eyebrows raised, but not in judgment. Rebecca swallowed before she continued. She knew corresponding with a gentleman one was not related to was scandalous, but she could not stop, not now the words were pouring from her soul.

"He did write back but see..." Pulling the letter once more from her reticule, she handed it over to Mrs. Dove-Lyon. "Since the brothers gained their titles, John has gained the name the Lennox Lion. All those ladies around him, all the time...he is like some sort of king with a pride of adoring ladies. Mrs. Dove-Lyon, I have sought to tame him over and over again, but I am always starting afresh, somehow."

"A lion who does not want to be caught," said Mrs. Dove-Lyon dryly.

Rebecca nodded. "I love him, Mrs. Dove-Lyon."

She needed John, and she knew he needed her, too, even if he did not yet understand it.

Mrs. Dove-Lyon's smile was that of a mother. "I know, dear, I can see it in your eyes. Do not concern yourself. We can help you."

"How?"

Mrs. Dove-Lyon spread her arms wide. "Welcome to the Lyon's Den, the place where gentlemen do what they are told, and ladies rule the roost."

Rebecca grinned despite her nerves. There was something very reassuring about Mrs. Dove-Lyon. Her establishment was famous, of course, but still...she did not really understand what occurred here. *How was it possible for Mrs. Dove-Lyon to make John realize he was in love with her?*

"And what happens now?"

Mrs. Dove-Lyon snapped her fingers, and the woman in breeches appeared from a door, holding a notebook and pencil.

"Now? We plan a little game."

JOHN WAS INITIALLY too focused on his breakfast to notice the post had come in.

In fairness, he thought, *it was a damned good breakfast.* His new cook—Mrs. Flutter, or Fitter, or whatever her name was—was a miracle worker. Even with the small budget he had allotted her, she made breakfasts for kings. He would have to up her budget. He would have to increase her salary, too.

It was only after finishing his poached eggs on toast that John started spreading butter onto two more pieces of toast and noticed the silver platter with a letter placed right by the butter dish.

Old Burnham must have come in with the post without him even noticing. John accidentally smeared jam over the envelope as he picked it up.

"Damn and blast!"

Trying to brush it clean had not been a wise idea. Now raspberry jam, all its little pips making dark pin marks on the paper, almost entirely covered the envelope.

Sighing heavily, John picked up his napkin and tried to get as much of the stickiness off his fingers, but to no avail. He was forced to disappear to his toilette, wash his hands, and then approach the letter as delicately as he could, cracking open the letter without touching the jam and paying no attention to the seal.

He had expected a letter. Instead, John pulled out a card that was entirely blank on one side. On the other side was printed writing.

John Lennox, Marquess of Gloucester

You have been chosen to attend the Lyon's Den on 15 February 18—at 6pm

Bring no one.

Leave all expectations at the door.

Cleveland Row, Whitehall

And that was it. Despite knowing the opposite side was blank, John turned it over in expectation of more details. A name, a reason he had been sent such a missive.

Nothing.

Stomach twisting, John leaned back in his chair. *The Lyon's Den.* He had heard of the exclusive club, of course. Every gentleman worth his salt had.

The rumors had swirled, details conflicting, and no one willing to declare they knew the absolute truth. If pressed, he was not sure he knew precisely what the place was, other than somewhere everyone wanted to go, and few received invitations for.

Why would he want to go? What happened there? He did not know a soul who had actually been there, after all, and it was not as though the card was signed.

Picking up the envelope, he examined the seal. L and D. *Well that made sense.* Lyon's Den. No other clues could be found.

John sighed. This was one to discuss with his brother.

Perhaps he had been there before.

Stretching and yawning as he rose, John paused only to pull a coat over his waistcoat, and then stepped into the brisk spring air. It was only two days away until the fifteenth, and spring's warmth had not yet arrived. William and Charlotte only lived a few doors down, and as he strode over to their front door, John did not even bother to knock.

"Do not worry yourself, Walters," John said breezily as the man stepped forward in the hallway, horrified his master's brother had entered unannounced. "I only dropped by for a quick word with William. Where is he?"

The butler drew himself up stiffly. "His Grace is in the breakfast room, but I warn you—"

"No need to warn me. I have seen him eat breakfast plenty of times," said John cheerfully.

In hindsight, he should have heeded the servant. John's mouth fell open as he stepped into the breakfast room to see a scene of absolute chaos.

Jam was smeared across the white linens on the table, with Charlotte at one end trying desperately to calm a screaming Elizabeth. John grinned at his niece. *Only six months old and already determined to make her opinion known.*

The other end of the table was just as hectic. William sat having a nonsensical conversation with his son—which shouldn't be surprising, considering that William the younger was only just over two years of age.

"No—no, William, do not put that in your—careful with that!"

John laughed. Long gone were their bachelor days together, when he and William would go about town, attending balls and leading relaxed lives.

"What is going on here?"

His brother turned his tired face to him, and little William squealed to see his favorite uncle.

"Nursemaid has some sort of illness," said the Duke of Mercia. "That woman is worth her weight in gold, but I only discovered such yesterday when she took to her bed. How does one get anything done with—no, not the teapot!"

Lurching forward to prevent his heir from scalding himself, William then collapsed back into his seat. The small child started running around the table.

"So, she has her bed, and you have these delights?" John could not help the joy in his voice. He loved his niece and nephew and would love all the others that came his way now both his sisters were married. *Still...what terrors!*

"Something like that," William sighed. "Grab the little man, will you?"

John reached for the toddler, who giggled furiously in his uncle's arms. "What do you think you are doing, little man, giving your father such a difficult time?"

Unabashed, the child giggled and flung his arms around him. "Jo-jo!"

"That is the problem with Pru getting married," said John as he sat down, keeping a firm grip on his nephew as Charlotte smiled. "Your reserve nursemaid is gone!"

Charlotte nodded. "I approve of her choice, of course, but it was rather inconveniently timed!"

John laughed. Prudence was the youngest Lennox and, in her

brothers' eyes, far too young to marry—even if she was near twenty years of age.

"I couldn't deny her, though a part of me wished to," William said heavily. "Anyone who can find someone in the world with whom to go through life is fortunate indeed, and she was welcome to that happiness once she had found it."

"Jojo," murmured little William softly.

John looked down to see the rambunctious boy falling asleep in his arms, already worn out by his adventures of the day. It was difficult not to feel a little jealous of his older brother.

The closest John had ever got to matrimony...

His heart twisted. *Miss Rebecca Darby.* There was a woman who was, in many ways, perfect for him. He had been enchanted with her beauty, there was a little wit there if you could find it in all the chattering, and her presence intoxicated him. *And yet...*

Something had held him back. Her company and beauty were perfect. But he couldn't...

John swallowed. He had forced himself to stop thinking about Miss Darby after he sent her that letter. If he was not going to propose marriage to her, he did not wish to be unfair. She needed to be free to find someone else.

Besides, contrary to public knowledge, the Marquess of Gloucester was a shy sort. Devilishly charming in public, naturally, but that was a carefully constructed persona.

"You want to talk to your brother." Charlotte's words cut through John's thoughts, and he looked up to see her examining him. "Come, let me take the children away, leave you two for your conversation."

"How did you know?" John asked.

Little William slipped off his lap and went to hold the hand of his mother, who smiled. "I was society's chaperone, do you not remember? If anyone knows what it looks like when two people want to talk alone, 'tis I."

After the door closed behind her, the breakfast room became strangely silent.

"Well? Is she right?"

John did not immediately respond. Instead, he pulled the invitation from his inside jacket pocket and handed it to his brother.

William whistled. "Well, well. The Lyon's Den. I have never received such an invitation. Will you attend?"

John hesitated before replying. He had felt utterly at sea when he received the invitation, but now the way seemed clear.

"I was not sure," he said honestly, "but if the Lion of the Lennoxes isn't brave enough to go into the Lyon's Den, who is?"

CHAPTER TWO

R EBECCA COULD NOT help it. Once again, her fingers moved to the
delicate ties around the back of her head that kept the mask—
gifted to her by Mrs. Dove-Lyon, although not until after the exchange
of six shillings—now hiding her identity.

It was absolutely vital no one recognized her.

That would be a disaster.

She watched the gambling floor below her, seated on the ladies'
observing gallery in the Lyon's Den. *It really was very cleverly designed*,
she thought to herself as her heart fluttered. The gambling floor was a
large space, almost like the Assembly Rooms in Bath, and yet from
here, similar to a minstrel's gallery, she could look out at the entire
space.

And there was an awful lot to watch. Thankful for the beautifully
designed gold and blue mask that hid her features and permitted her to
not only look but stare, Rebecca tried to take in the splendor and
majesty that was the Lyon's Den.

It was a terrifying world she had never known. *Who could have
guessed that such a place existed—and in London, too!*

While her soul whispered she still did not know whether she

would go through with it, Rebecca sat quietly.

The gambling floor had several different tables. Most were round, but a few were square, designed for close, intimate games.

Gentlemen were everywhere. Loud, rowdy gentlemen. Quiet, brooding gentlemen. Some of them looked a little worse for wear for drink. Others looked captivated by the game on their table, but Rebecca, try as she might, struggled to fully understand the games.

At one, a woman was throwing a knife at the table, and any man who removed his hand was considered "out." It looked dangerous, and there was more than one man with serious-looking cuts on his fingers.

At another table, each man was taking a mouthful of a disgusting-looking stew, and as one vomited, the others cheered. Rebecca curled up her nose. She could not imagine inviting that sort of sickness into one's body—and yet the gentleman who had vomited looked...pleased. Rebecca's mouth fell open—though no sound came out—as he was presented with some sort of token, and a lady, who was evidently one of Mrs. Dove-Lyon's ladies, came to convey him to another table.

Was...was he the winner then?

It was all so confusing. Rebecca shook her head slightly, as though ridding water from her ears. Mrs. Dove-Lyon had explained much of it to her, but it was difficult to understand. Gentlemen always were.

They came here, willingly, understanding they may leave the place with a wife they had never met before, and to gain her would subject themselves to...*well*.

They were strange beasts.

Rebecca's gaze drifted to a third table. Upon it was a cage, and within it, a snake, curling its lengths around and around as the gentlemen watched it. They were unusually silent.

She looked away. She did not consider herself to be particularly squeamish, but even she had limits. There was no chance she wished to know what would happen at that table.

Mrs. Dove-Lyon had been right, though.

"You will find that though gentlemen rule the world outside, in my Lyon's Den, 'tis the ladies who rule the roost."

Rebecca swallowed. It was intoxicating to be in the presence of such power, and from ladies, too. She did not think she had ever seen so many women in charge of anything.

Moreover, the gentlemen appeared to be accustomed to it. There they were, taking orders from women they would not look twice at if on the street and would perhaps actively ignore if they met at a ball.

Rebecca's gaze was caught by a movement to her left. She was not alone. Five or six other ladies, all wearing masks of different colors, were seated along the railing of the gallery, all looking down at the gentlemen playing their games.

A lady in Lyon's Den apparel had come up the stairs and was whispering in the ear of another of the masked ladies. Rebecca could not help but watch.

What was happening?

Rebecca swallowed. There was more than one plot occurring here tonight, and if they were all fortunate, all would leave here with a gentleman.

Would she?

"Titania?"

Rebecca jumped, turning to see another of Mrs. Dove-Lyon's ladies smiling. She was wearing the most incredible gown she had ever seen—more lace and embroidery, more diamonds sewn into the fabric than she had believed possible.

Titania. That was the codename Mrs. Dove-Lyon had given her. She had almost forgotten, in her obsessive viewing of the gentlemen below.

The woman was smiling. "Do not concern yourself, Titania. We do not use real names here. We are discretion itself. You may call me Hermia."

Rebecca nodded, sure she would simply not remember. *A Mid-*

summer Night's Dream, then? It seemed fitting. Half of this seemed a nightmare, the other half-dream.

"I am one of Mrs. Dove-Lyon's ladies, and she wished me to inform you that your dream is almost ready," said Hermia with a grin. "You will be signaled by her in a moment, and then it will begin. You must prepare yourself for excitement, for power—and for the game."

Before Rebecca could reply that she was not ready, and perhaps it would be better if she just went home, Hermia had disappeared.

Rebecca had not seen her move. She had simply melted into the distance, which did nothing to calm her nerves.

Catching the eye of the lady seated beside her, she looked at her hands in her lap. She needed to stay calm, that was all.

Swallowing, she lifted her gaze to the gambling floor. Newly arriving gentlemen were walking in, one with his head held high as though he had been here a thousand times before, the others looking nervous.

Only when one of them looked up curiously did Rebecca gasp. *It was John.*

JOHN FOUGHT THE instinct to rub his eyes to ensure he was not dreaming. The impulse was strong. Places like this simply did not exist. *Not in London. Not in England.*

And yet, here he was. After being ushered through a lounge and then a smoking room packed with noise and smoke that stung the eyes, he was standing in a large room with a high ceiling that did not seem to be of this world.

None of it could be real; the wild costumes beggared belief, there was music coming from somewhere, but he could not fathom where—and the smells...

No, if he were unsure whether this was real or some sort of wine-induced dream, the smells alone would persuade him this was reality. No dream could smell like this: the heaving scent of too many gentlemen all in one place for far too long.

John walked past a table of gentlemen guessing how many cards a woman was holding, the loser removing a piece of clothing if he was the furthest from the truth.

He shook his head, moving around other tables.

Was that—was that a snake in a cage on that table? John's stomach lurched, and he increased his pace. He could accept some strange strip game; he could accept the smoking room and its noise and chatter— but not snakes. *No, thank you.*

The next table caught his attention for a few minutes. There was some sort of fascinating knife throwing game, and only when one man pulled away his hand too soon did the table erupt with laughter.

"I am sorry, sir, you know the rules," said the lady with the knife, expertly flicking it from one hand to the other. "Goodbye."

The gentleman picked up his jacket with very poor grace as his companions jeered. Beneath the jeers, even he could see, was relief it had not been them.

John swallowed. He was not entirely sure whether this was the sort of place for him. He had imagined it being full of beautiful women, and though there were women here, they were in charge and hardly dressed for the delight of their guests.

A pleasure palace. That was what the Lyon's Den was. A place where gamblers were made of the strangest kind, and where gentle-men could find wives who were a little more wild and bold than the typical fare one found at Almack's.

That was what he had heard—but then, what had he not heard?
Marriages.

As he turned a corner, his gaze drifted upward—and was rewarded by the view of the sort of ladies he had expected. There an observing gallery, a balustrade keeping him from seeing the ladies properly, but just enough to catch a glimpse.

His stomach clenched. Each wore a gown elegantly torn to reveal far more skin than would ever have been permitted at Almack's. Each wore a mask, cleverly hiding their faces.

Only then did he realize his mouth was open. John shut it hurriedly before someone noticed. He had been invited here, and that could only mean one thing.

There was a lady up there, one of those looking down at him like some sort of empress, who wanted him here—*who wanted him.*

Now, a piece of card was carefully folded in his waistcoat pocket that gave him access to a world of pleasure, and perhaps a wife.

It was a heady thought. That simply didn't happen in society; it was the men that chased the women. It was thrilling, intoxicating.

Courting, matrimony...he had only given serious thought to them when he had met...

He would not think about Rebecca Darby, not here. Though his heart contracted painfully, and he had to force away the memory of her face, he would not think of her.

He had not been brave enough. He was certain to have lost her now to a better man, no doubt.

He had the chance now to find a wife with none of the complications. Perhaps that was best. He simply did not have the stomach to court and woo a lady. Flirt, yes. Jest. Quiz. Laugh. *But attempting to convince her to...*

Again, he forced his mind away from Miss Darby. There were plenty of things before him, after all, to keep his mind occupied.

There were the gentlemen. Most of them he did not recognize, but there were a few faces known to him.

There, on the snake table, was the Earl of Marnmouth. *Philip Egerton, wasn't it?* The man looked utterly bored out of his mind, which was certainly not the emotional state he would have been with such a creature so close to him.

Spying an empty table at the edge of the room, John made toward it as calmly as he could manage and collapsed gratefully into a chair.

What did he think he was doing here? This was not a place for the likes of him. He had neither the stomach nor the bravery for it, and everywhere he looked, there was something dangerous, or wild, or worse—heavenly.

He glanced up at the gallery once more. There were fewer ladies now. Evidently, some had found the gentlemen they sought and were secreted away somewhere else in the building.

Who could want him here?

"Ah, the Lennox Lion."

John jumped. A woman dressed in the most ostentatious excuse for a gown he had ever seen was standing beside him. She had been so silent, he had not even noticed her approach.

He smiled nervously. "That is what they call me, though I cannot profess to know why, Miss...?"

The woman did not offer her name. "I presume you were so named because of your harem of ladies."

John's cheeks flushed. "Harem? My dear lady, I do not think I would describe—"

"A jest, of course," interrupted the lady with a knowing smile. "I have watched you, John Lennox, out in the world. So cheerful, so bold. Always ready with a laugh, a joke, a jest. Always a lady on your arm. And yet, I think, a heart untouched."

John opened his mouth to speak, but no words came. *What on earth did this woman want with him?* She was part of the establishment—no mask—so did that give her the right to speak to him in that way?

The fact she was correct was neither here nor there.

"I suppose that is where the name came from then, yes," he said stiffly. "And no serious connections, no."

He would not tell this harlot about Rebecca—Miss Darby. No, she was a secret in his heart that he would keep to himself. None of them deserved to even know of her.

Besides, none of the ladies which he jested with in the dances or laughed with at the card tables would ever consider appearing here, surely. This was a place of iniquity, even if that was utterly consented to by its patrons.

And the idea that Rebecca would be here...

John smiled despite himself. She *was* the only lady who had ever touched his heart, and his smile grew wistful as he thought of her. *If only he had been brave enough to offer for her.*

But he had not. The idea of committing, forever, to one woman—what if it had been the wrong choice? What if they were not compatible in...well, other ways? What if, worst of all, she had refused him?

John coughed. "You are one of Mrs. Dove-Lyon's ladies, are you not?"

The woman smiled. "I am, and you may call me Hermia. Have a pleasant evening, Lennox Lion."

In a sweep of skirts, she was gone.

Hermia. A Midsummer Night's Dream—it made sense. The more he looked around the room, the more John realized that each table was managed by a woman.

Women in charge. Well, it was a new world they were creating in England, at any rate, and so it should not have surprised him to find such things here.

He knew plenty of gentlemen who could barely get their own boots on, whereas every lady he knew seemed to run a home, host parties, organize the kitchen, embroider, sing, speak two languages...

Perhaps he should be more surprised to find a gentleman in charge than a lady.

There was a rustle of skirts this time to announce a lady's approach, and this one was a little older but no less majestic as the last one.

"John 'the Lion' Lennox, is it?" she said stiffly. "You may kiss my hand."

For an instant, John thought she was joking, but the woman held out her hand imperiously. Unsure whether this was a game, a gamble, or some sort of strange rite of passage, John nevertheless reached out and kissed the woman's hand.

And then she was all smiles. "I like you, John. May I call you John?"

"I-I suppose so," he spluttered, utterly at sea. He was not accustomed to feeling so lost in a conversation—*who was this one?* "And I may call you...?"

The woman raised an eyebrow. "Mrs. Dove-Lyon, the proprietress of the Lyon's Den."

John rose to his feet and bowed low. *Damn and blast it. He had not even thought that a woman like this had to be in charge. Of course she did!*

She laughed. "Yes, yes, that is all very well. But the night is growing older, John, and so am I. Would you like to play a special game I have for you?"

CHAPTER THREE

T HE BREATH THAT filled Rebecca's lungs was sharp, but perhaps that was the panic, not the air itself.

That was the signal. There had been no mistaking it, even from up here in the observing gallery. She had been told by Mrs. Dove-Lyon what to expect, and she had watched the empress of an owner walk carefully toward John, approaching him as a hunter did its prey.

Silently.

Rebecca had almost laughed when she watched John start. But now it was time for her to act. *Time for her to do something.* Because all this hard work, fear, panic—let alone the number of guineas which had changed hands—would all be for nothing if she did not stand up right now.

It was with some surprise that Rebecca found her legs were, after all, strong enough to carry her. If she had not known better, she would have said they were shaking from the panic and excitement flowing through her veins.

Was she really about to do this?

This was not what young ladies did. This was not a place where young ladies came.

Yet, she was not alone here on the observational gallery. Rebecca looked to her left and right at the other masked ladies waiting in their turn for their signal from Mrs. Dove-Lyon.

"Good luck," the nearest whispered. There was fear and excitement in her voice.

Rebecca nodded. She did not have the breath nor the words to speak, but she felt the solidarity of the unknown woman, and it heartened her as nothing else had.

A few others whispered words of encouragement as she slowly stepped past them and toward the stairs. For a moment, Rebecca was tempted to halt and ask if they had advice, any idea what was going to happen next.

Surely some of them were Mrs. Dove-Lyon's ladies and not ladies like herself with absolutely no idea what was going on?

Perhaps they were all like her—completely out of their depth and unsure exactly what was going to happen next.

As Rebecca reached the stairs, her grip on the banister earthed her as nothing else had. This piece of wood, tangible and warm, was real. It was something she could quite literally hold onto for a minute, to remind herself this was a real place.

Her steps faltered, her heart racing. *What was she doing? What if this all went wrong? What if,* and she swallowed in panic at the very thought of it, *what if John did not even wish to play the game at all?*

At the bottom of the stairs was Hermia. She was not smiling but had a rather grim look on her face, as though she was a general about to send a soldier into battle.

"Come on now, Titania," she said firmly. "Down you come."

Rebecca nodded mutely and continued down the last few steps. She had reached the bottom. Her feet stood on solid ground, and she removed her fingers from the safety of the banister.

Hermia nodded. "Go and get him."

Rebecca laughed nervously—she could not help it. In some ways, this was all a game.

Yet there was nothing pretend about the gambling floor as she stepped onto it.

Wolf whistles rang out in the air, coupled with laughter and a few slaps on the back to force gentlemen to pay attention to the game before them.

Rebecca held her head up high. Somehow, their delight in her appearance was the spark needed to make her brave. It was rather thrilling in a way, and she felt a little more as though she belonged.

It was not difficult to guess where the wolf whistles came from. The gown she had been given by Mrs. Dove-Lyon had made her laugh at first until she realized the proprietress was quite serious in her wearing it.

It was ridiculous. It was the wildest thing she had ever seen, and yet when Rebecca had carefully been tied into it, a rush of power had flowed through her veins.

There was something rather freeing about wearing a gown torn in all the right places, low in the bodice, and high in the leg.

Absolutely not something she would ever wear in public. It was the sort of thing Mrs. Bryant, society's gossip, would have called "wanton."

And it was. But somehow, Rebecca found more power in it than any of her delicate muslin gowns so carefully made for her.

In short, Rebecca found that her hips swung a little more than usual. Her head was held higher. A smile danced across her lips, and it became a laugh as heads turned, one man's mouth dropped open.

She continued to ignore the stares, her gaze now fixed on someone else entirely.

John.

He was on the other side of the room as she slowly made her way around, and the closer she got, the more her heart started to thunder.

All she had to do was be patient. Not an unusual recommendation to a lady, Rebecca thought dryly, but a little galling all the same, when she had been waiting for John for almost two years.

Delicately lowering herself into a seat at the table along from his, Rebecca tried not to show her nerves. Her hands were folded in her lap, so she could not fiddle with her hair or mask, and she resolutely looked in another direction.

It was no good. In her peripheral vision, she could still see John, and more importantly, could see he was eying her with great interest.

"Be restrained," Mrs. Dove-Lyon had said in their preparatory talk what felt like an age ago. *"You must demonstrate he has to earn your attention. It would never do to give John the feeling that he had the upper hand, after all."*

Rebecca smiled at the memory of those words. Mrs. Dove-Lyon spoke as though gentlemen were...not strictly inferior. More to be cared for, like children. They could not look after themselves and certainly could not find wives of their own volition.

It was down to ladies like Mrs. Dove-Lyon to make sure gentlemen got there in the end.

Plenty of other gentlemen were now staring. One nudged his companion, who was too occupied by the game to notice her, and they both gawped.

Perhaps, a voice whispered in her heart, *they are wondering whether you are the lady who has brought them here. Maybe they are hoping you are.*

It was a heady thought. To be so desired; it was not something, as Miss Darby, she had ever experienced.

The table nearest her had fallen silent, all save for one of the gentlemen.

"—is she, do you know, Helena?"

The woman running the table looked majestic, and Rebecca tried to keep her eyes averted as she replied to the inquiring gentleman.

"Not for you. That's who she is."

Rebecca's smile was small, but she could not force it down.

No one acted like this for little Becky Darby.

There was a swish of skirts, and Rebecca found herself being addressed by Mrs. Dove-Lyon with a serious look.

"Are you ready?"

"What, now?" Rebecca said foolishly, her mouth opening before she could take a moment to think.

Mrs. Dove-Lyon frowned. "Do not lose heart so quickly, *Titania*. You have much further to go than this."

There was such truth in her words Rebecca was forced to take a deep breath to calm her stuttering nerves.

She was right. This was the doorway to her adventure, and she was about to step through it. Once she went beyond this point, there was no way back.

Only in that moment did she realize she did not want to go back. She wanted John, and if this was the best way to get him, then she would go forward. She would never be able to live with herself if she did not try everything.

Then, if it did not work… The sudden sharp pain of the thought made her gasp. A life without John. She would not even permit it to occur.

Mrs. Dove-Lyon was watching her carefully. "Well?"

Rebecca nodded. "I am ready."

She barely noticed the owner of the Lyon's Den leaving her side. The next thing she knew, the woman was speaking to John—quietly, but clearly enough for Rebecca to hear.

"Would you like to play a game?"

There was some sort of drumming in the room, and Rebecca looked around swiftly for it—only to realize it was the pounding of her heartbeat in her ears.

"A game?" John said curiously, a smile dancing on his face. "What kind of game?"

There was laughter around them. Others had heard Mrs. Dove-Lyon's words.

"Go for it, my son," said one of the gentlemen with a leer. "If you have the chance to play one of Mrs. Dove-Lyon's games, you go for it!"

"I have been here months and have never been invited to my own game," said another, a little wistfully. "A bride is waiting in the wings, man, and one specially chosen for you!"

A third laughed. "Just make sure you understand what happens if you lose, though—some of the forfeits here are criminal!"

Rebecca glanced at John to see his reaction. To her surprise, his smile had slipped. She had never known him to be unsure of himself in any situation. He was the Lion of the Lennoxes, never showing fear. He was typically the one teasing someone else.

But this was different.

"Ignore the rabble, sir," said Mrs. Dove-Lyon imperiously. Her words wiped the smiles off the faces of those who had spoken, and they turned back to their tables hastily. "Just concentrate on me, sir. Now, 'tis very simple. A guessing game."

Despite her desire to remain calm and aloof, Rebecca could not help twisting her fingers in her lap. Yes, a guessing game. She and Mrs. Dove-Lyon had agreed on it as one of the most straightforward approaches to their plan.

Anything too complicated, and Rebecca was concerned she may not adequately manage it. If she was going to win John's heart, once and for all, then the game they played together needed to be something she could control, even when she thought she would die of love for him.

In the heat of the moment, it was quite possible she would lose her head, especially when so close to him. *Breathing in his scent. Close enough to touch him...*

Rebecca shook her head. Loving John was dangerous, and on more than one occasion, she had found herself speaking absolute nonsense just to fill the silence, unable to just stand and look at him.

She loved him, and he knew that. Any fool would have known it; she was hardly subtle! Her stomach twisted at the memory of some of the nonsense she had said, the letter she had written him...

Yet, he had not returned her affection. *If she could just get him to see her differently, to see her in a different light...*

John was smiling—not at her, but at Mrs. Dove-Lyon. "A guessing game, eh? Well, that seems easy enough. What are the rules?"

"Nothing too arduous, I assure you," said Mrs. Dove-Lyon smoothly.

Rebecca could not comprehend how she was able to speak so calmly. *Did she not know she held the power to make or break Rebecca's happiness?*

"You win, you get the girl. You lose, and she can do anything she wishes with you," said Mrs. Dove-Lyon quietly, her gaze not leaving John.

This was the culmination of their plans, and they could do no more to ensure her happiness.

If all went well, this was the moment where the rest of her life began.

If it went against her hopes and expectations...

"I am happy to play this game of yours, Mrs. Dove-Lyon, with pleasure," said John cheerfully. "At which table is this game being played?"

Rebecca found she had been holding her breath and allowed the air out of her lungs. He had agreed. The game would be played. She would win him; she knew she would.

For the first time, she lost control and turned her head to look over at his table. John was still seated, smiling, and looking around the room to espy a guessing game table. Mrs. Dove-Lyon, on the other hand, looked just as majestic as ever.

"No table, sir, no table for you," she said quietly. "This is a very special game, and that means you have your own special room."

The gentlemen who had turned their backs had continued to eavesdrop, for cheers went up at the owner's words.

"His own room?"

"Lucky devil, I've been coming here for three months, and I've never had an invitation to a room!"

"And on his first time, too," said one with an envious look.

"Someone must have their eye on you, my lad!"

Rebecca's cheeks heated, but the gambling floor, lit only by a few candles, was thankfully dim enough to hide her emotions. No one could see her embarrassment—and of course, they could not possibly know she was the one who planned this. Mrs. Dove-Lyon never revealed her secrets nor her sources, and that meant ladies could come to the Lyon's Den with the secure knowledge that she would act on their behalf whilst never betraying them.

John rose. "Well, it appears I have hit the jackpot! Please lead on, Mrs. Dove-Lyon. I will play this game with one of your delightful ladies."

For the first time in their conversation, Mrs. Dove-Lyon smiled. "Yes. Yes, you will."

She took him by the hand and pulled him along, the cheers of the gentlemen nearest them echoing.

Rebecca was careful not to watch as Mrs. Dove-Lyon took him to one of the private rooms at the end of the gambling floor. It was vital no one could connect the two of them. Not now, everything was in motion for the most scandalous night of her life.

It was impossible to steady her breathing, but she attempted it, nonetheless. Until now, there had always been a way back, but no longer. John had agreed to it, and he was in that room, waiting for her—though he did not know it.

Everything had been prepared, painstakingly agonized over to ensure her success. She had been most precise with Mrs. Dove-Lyon, and she could see now she was a woman to be trusted.

All she had to do now was keep her wits and seduce John. How hard could it be?

"Ready?"

Rebecca jumped. Once again, Mrs. Dove-Lyon demonstrated her ability to move silently.

She nodded, rising to her feet. "I am ready to tame the Lion of the Lennoxes."

CHAPTER FOUR

JOHN BARELY HAD time to register where he was, pushed as he was by Mrs. Dove-Lyon from behind, before the door closed behind him. He was alone, in a room he had no time to examine, about to play a game he did not quite understand where he could win...*a woman?*

The shyness he had always pushed down and ignored swelled in his gut, and he coughed in the awkward silence to dispel it.

The room was not, after all, that unusual. It was set out as a bedchamber, with nothing particularly strange within it. *More a woman's boudoir than a bedchamber*, he noticed as his eyes took in the furniture.

A desk with a chair, ornate wood, and delicate upholstery. A wardrobe in the same wood, carvings at the corners that matched a small chest of drawers. Two armchairs with the same blue satin upholstery sat on either side of the bed.

The bed. It should not have been a surprise. He had heard enough rumors about the Lyon's Den to know what sort of things occurred here—always between willing participants, as far as he had heard, but still.

Lovemaking. Wild, wanton pleasure. Decadent sensuality.

The mere thoughts were enough to make him shiver. In all his years, and probably much to the surprise of his friends, if they had found out, John had never visited a brothel.

After what happened to Honora, he never would. He had heard enough stories to be sickened at the very thought of it.

She would recover in time, and she had married well. William may not have liked him at first, but they put up with each other, and that was all most brothers-in-law could hope for.

But finding Honora there, against her will…

John had vowed never to go near such a place. He would never subject a woman who was there unwillingly to his own desires.

If this was such a place, he would not remain long.

Besides, despite all of his laughter with William and his friends, he had never quite managed to…

John coughed into the silence once more. Standing here alone was disorientating, strange. Was there not supposed to be a woman to play the game with him? He swallowed down his rising panic and moved about the room a bit.

Well, she was not to know he had never lain with a woman. His innocence had never been lost, not as a soldier, nor as a gentleman when he had come into his rather surprising title.

It was a secret he had never shared, and now it appeared he would have to admit it. This woman who was about to enter the room—she would surely be more experienced than he, wouldn't she?

Not that it would be hard, John thought bitterly. *What had he managed to get himself into?*

The guessing game the woman had suggested made it appear there was no way to lose—either he won himself a bride, or she could do whatever she wanted with him, which sounded highly suggestive. But his bravado on the gaming floor melted away as he stood looking at the bed. It was made up beautifully, but there could be no confusion about what it was for.

What had Mrs. Dove-Lyon said?

"No table, sir, no table for you. This is a very special game, and that *means you have your own special room."*

Well, it appeared that unless he thought the lady—when she appeared—was under coercion, that innocence he had kept for so many years would be lost this evening.

John found himself hoping fervently that if it was so, then the lady would be pretty, as well as able to string a sentence together. He had no doubt Mrs. Dove-Lyon chose ladies of excellent beauty, but if she was dull and beautiful, he would find it difficult to—

The thought died as the door opened and closed quickly, allowing a burst of laughter and noise to seep in. And then it was gone, leaving only the new occupant of the room, who was leaning against the door.

John's heart—and manhood—lurched painfully. *Perhaps this game was not such a bad idea at all.*

It was the lady who had been seated at the table beside his. He had noticed her, of course, he had. He was only human, and there was plenty of her to look at. The gown was torn artfully, designed at its very core to reveal rather than conceal.

Even under the mask, he could see she was beautiful. Bright sparkling eyes, a smile that danced across her lips and seemed to tease him. But beyond that, there was an elegance about her that poured from every inch of her skin—and there was quite a lot of it on display.

As she took a step toward him, the gown shifted and revealed even more skin—enough to get John's heart racing.

His hands felt clammy, his heart thundered, and his throat seemed to be closing up. She was beautiful. She was the most beautiful woman he had ever seen, and he had entertained a fair few.

"Well, you are the gentleman I have been given, then," she said lightly. "I suppose I shall have to make the best of you."

Her confidence was electrifying, and John found himself grinning at her jest—or at least, what he hoped was her jest. After being so impressed with her, it would be sad indeed if she was disappointed with him.

"Yes," he said in a rather strangled voice. "I mean, I hope so. You are so…"

John's voice trailed away, and he cursed his shyness for rearing its head just when he needed to be the suave Lennox Lion he had come to depend on.

The lady laughed. "Do not concern yourself, sir. I know precisely how I look. Come, why do you not sit on a chair for me? Bring it here, in the middle of the room."

John nodded, obedience kicking in at such a commanding tone. *How could he argue?* This woman, whoever she was, had evidently performed such things before. Her confidence oozed into every word. He was clearly not the first gentleman she had ordered about.

He moved the chair into the center of the room and sat on it.

"My name is John," he said, gazing at her. "What may I call you?"

"Me?"

If John did not know any better, he would have guessed she was surprised at his question.

"They call me Titania," she said, tilting her head. "But you can call me the Lion Tamer."

She wanted him. There was hunger in her eyes.

This entire game had been planned, and he was, as one of the men at the tables had said, damned lucky.

Well, he would have to give her what she asked for.

Titania stepped around him, circling him as a hunter circled prey. "Why are you nervous? Am I frightening?"

There was a hint of amusement in her words but no mockery.

Titania ended her circle, standing before him, and John tried to force down the attraction.

"Consider me your confessor," she said in a low voice. "Whatever you tell me will never leave my lips."

John found himself staring at her lips before coughing and saying, "Well, I am no fool, and I know what is likely to occur here. And I have not…I have never…not before. Not with anyone."

Why in God's name were his cheeks heating up—were they visibly red?

And yet, the shame he had expected to flow through him did not arrive. Somehow, sharing this with the masked Titania was like sharing it with a priest. He knew, trusted, that she would tell no others.

"You surprise me."

"I have fallen in love, once," John found himself saying. "But…"

Titania tilted her head again. "You are unmarried."

John nodded. "I was not man enough to tell her how I felt. I am a shy soul. I did nothing about the affection I felt, more fool me."

REBECCA COULD NOT believe her ears. This was not happening. It was not true—was it?

John Lennox, the Marquess of Gloucester, the man about town, the gentleman every lady wished to flirt with…

A virgin?

He was just as innocent as she, though she found it difficult to understand how on earth that could be true. The way he acted with the ladies of the ton, the way he spoke, so practiced in the arts of seduction, *that particularly delightful way he had of kissing her just below the ear…*

Rebecca shivered and hoped he had not noticed. *Was he genuinely saying that he had never made love to a woman?*

It was a heady thought, the idea that she could be the first woman to ever tame the lion who stalked about society, looking as though he ate young ladies for breakfast.

If she played her cards right—if, and the thought prompted a little smile, *if she could play this game right, she would be the first. They would be each other's firsts.*

John was smiling. "You are shocked."

Rebecca did not permit herself to speak at first but merely matched his smile.

"I am not surprised. I thought you would be," he said quietly. "Which part shocks you more, that I am utterly innocent, or that I have been in love, or that I did not do anything about it?"

Her instinct to inquire further about this mysterious woman he had mentioned, the one woman he had fallen in love with, was forced down. She needed to remain in control of herself. *If she gave herself away—if he guessed who she was...*

"All of it," she said.

John laughed, that chuckle she knew so well. *Had she not made him laugh before, a hundred times?*

"Well, that is a true enough answer, I suppose," he said ruefully. "And here I was, hoping I would be able to impress you!"

John, looking to impress her?

How the tables had turned. Would he feel ridiculous for saying such things when he was eventually told who she was?

She tried not to think about it. It was far easier to continue on with her plan if she did not have to think of the consequences of what must happen at the end. It was critical, in short, that she simply carried on with what Mrs. Dove-Lyon had instructed her to do.

With a few embellishments of her own, naturally.

Continuing her slow walk around him, allowing him to see various angles of her that he may not have before, Rebecca tried to think—or more accurately, not think—about this mysterious woman who had captured John's heart.

He was in love with someone. She could hear the plaintive notes in his voice, even if he did not realize he had betrayed himself. The small, strong hope it was she he had been speaking of was foolish, she knew. John Lennox had never looked at her like that.

Besides, if she had been the one to catch his eye, he had had plenty of opportunities to win her heart, to ask for it—she would have handed it over immediately.

So, he was speaking of someone else. Rebecca felt the anger rise in her heart, but once again, she forced down any strong emotions.

Another woman? Fine. She would soon change that. She would make him forget about her. Rebecca was certain she would do anything, allow him to do anything if it meant he would forget this undeserving woman.

"Well, you have your chance to impress me now," she said quietly, moving to face him once more. "We are here to play a game, aren't we? Remember, if you win, you win me. You lose, and you are in my power."

"I think I am in your power already."

His voice was a little hoarse, and she savored seeing the desire in John's features. He certainly was, and it made her feel as though she could fly to the rooftops and sing out her love.

The power was intoxicating. *Why had she not done this a long time ago? Why had she not sought Mrs. Dove-Lyon a year ago?*

"I understand the rules of this game of yours, or at least I think I do," said John quietly into the silence. "And I think it only fair to tell you, Titania, that I do not think I care whether I win or lose. I think I win either way."

Rebecca's heart sang. *He wanted her; this was going to work!* She was going to win John as her husband.

But she could not begin, not yet. John said he understood, and the large bed certainly told part of the story. But it was not the story in its entirety, and she had to ensure he understood it all—or her efforts would be for nothing.

"You…you do not know who I am, do you?" Her voice was hesitant, questioning.

John shook his head. "No, my lady, though I admit I wish I had made your acquaintance outside of here, in the real world. What fun we could have had."

He was smiling, sure of his compliment, but his words pained

35

Rebecca. He did not recognize her, which was to the good—but it was a little disheartening that after over a year of acquaintance, after balls and operas and walks and carriage rides, after kisses stolen in the rain and in gardens…

After all that, John Lennox did not connect the attractive and alluring woman who stood before him with the chattering Miss Darby with whom he had spent so much time.

"You do not know me, and yet you are willing to play a gambling game to win my hand?" Rebecca said quietly. She watched John carefully. *He had to understand.* "Do not misunderstand me—if you win, you marry me."

If he dissented, said he did not realize the severity of the gamble in the game, requested to leave—she would let him. Her heart would break, but she would allow him through the door.

If, on the other hand, he agreed…

John swallowed. "One of the biggest challenges I face, Titania, is that I am…I am shy."

Rebecca laughed aloud and felt immediately guilty as pain crossed his face. "I do apologize, I just…John Lennox, shy? I am not sure whether you are jesting or in earnest."

But she could now see the answer on his face.

"I would never have guessed that about you," she continued.

John leaned back in the armchair. "No one does—because I hide it well. Shy gentlemen do not get anywhere in life, and so I have had to work hard at ensuring I am never found out."

It was a revelation Rebecca had never expected. *John Lennox, shy! In truth, as shy as she was!*

Was it possible—had they both been circling each other, wanting to speak but held back by their shyness?

"You say if I succeed, I win your hand. Good," said John quietly. "I do not think I will ever have the courage to ask a woman to marry me, so if you…if you like me, then why not?"

It was not precisely the ringing endorsement she had hoped for, nor the declaration of love she had once believed she would receive.

But it was something. It was the only way to secure him, and her love only grew as she beheld him. Her lion, the man who had utterly stolen her heart—just as bashful as she was.

They were made for each other.

"Well then," she said softly. "Let the game begin. If you are ready."

CHAPTER FIVE

"*IF YOU ARE ready.*"

Ready? Ready for a game that would, in all likelihood, end with him becoming the future husband of the delectable woman who stood before him?

He had never been less ready—and yet the panic and regret he had assumed would tear through his heart had not appeared. If anything, quite the opposite. He felt calm, his breathing steady.

Once he was committed to this, and he was dancing along the edge of that commitment now, there was no going back.

It suggested there was a connection between them, something intangible but real.

His closely guarded secret had been laid out before her, and she had not considered him a fool for not being experienced.

He desperately wanted her. *Every inch of him craved her, the way she looked at him so boldly, her smile, her laugh…*

He was ready to leave behind his bachelor ways. A life with Titania had to be better than the solitary life he had.

"I am ready," he said quietly.

"Excellent. Now we will—"

"But first, I would like to ask you a few questions," John said.

Titania had evidently not been expecting that. She had started toward the chest of drawers but hesitated.

"I will not tell you my real name if that is what you are after," she said with a dazzling smile. "That is something you may earn at the end of the game, of course."

John nodded. He had wanted to ask, in truth, but had guessed she would not tell him. "I only wondered…playing this game may lead to us being very important to each other for a very long time. I wanted to know a little about you—not your name, obviously—before we began. Is that acceptable?"

He had attempted to pour a little of the Lennox Lion charm into the last sentence, and to his delight, he saw Titania's cheeks pink. *So, she was not immune to him, either.*

"What is it you would like to know?" she said cautiously.

John considered for a moment. "'Tis the month of Valentine's Day. If you were not here, where would you be?"

He had not considered it an impertinent question, and yet Titania hesitated before she replied. There was some sort of internal battle going on within her.

"I would be with my family, probably," she said eventually, her gaze not entirely meeting his own. "I have no beau if that is what you are inquiring about."

It was, though John would not admit it.

"Brothers, sisters?"

Titania, or whatever her name was, hesitated once more before she said, "None."

John nodded, now at his limits of ideas of questions. *How was he supposed to understand this woman if he could not ask some of the most basic questions about a person?*

Well, answered a small voice in his head, *ask the questions that are not basic.*

"Do you like opera?"

Titania had been walking around the room again, but she stumbled on something—a corner of the rug, perhaps?—at his words.

"What did you say?"

John heard the panic in her voice but could not understand it. *Opera was hardly a taboo subject, was it?*

"Opera or theatre," he said quietly. "I just...by God, I am attracted to you, Titania. I am happy to admit it, but I want a partnership, too, Titania, a collaboration to make us both happy."

She had moved now to sit at the chair by the desk. John attempted not to look at the way her thighs became more visible by the way she crossed her legs.

"Here you are, with a beautiful woman about to offer herself to you through a game," she said quietly. "And you wish to understand my preferences in music?"

John nodded with a wry smile. "I suppose I am not like most of the other visitors to the Lyon's Den."

"John Lennox, you are the most singular, the most unique..." Titania's voice trailed off as she stared, and John felt his heart quicken.

She knew him well, then. *But did that mean he knew her—had they met, under different names, under different circumstances?* Had his gaze flickered past her without him realizing it?

There was something familiar in that smile. If he were not in a room in the Lyon's Den about to play a seductive teasing game with a masked woman, he would have said...*but no, it was impossible.*

Rebecca Darby would never be found in a place like this.

"I love opera and mussels, and the way starlings flock in the autumn," Titania said softly. "You like opera, but you do not love it. You prefer concerts—Mozart, mainly. You adore cards, but you are not very good. Yet you never cheat."

John found his mouth falling open. "You—you know me well, Titania."

Her smile became a little more assured at his words. "I am not called the Lyon Tamer for nothing, John. Now, you have a little more knowledge of me. Are you ready to play?"

John nodded. He could not delay any longer—not when his body was desperate for them to get closer.

Titania did not seem to need him to move. Instead, she rose herself, moving elegantly to the chest of drawers in the corner. She pulled open a drawer, positioning that rather delicious behind between them so he could not see what she was doing.

John's mind raced back to the tables he had wandered past in the gambling room, and only then did he wonder whether this whole excursion had been a mistake.

He was hardly a daredevil! His time in the army as a soldier had seen no battle, and he had never been in a duel in his life.

What was she about to bring out for this game—this guessing game? Snakes? Knives? *Something worse?*

What could the Lion Tamer do with him?

Titania pulled something from the drawer, and for a heart-wrenching moment, he thought it was a snake.

And then he blinked and saw it for what it was—a blindfold.

"There it is," she said softly.

Straightening up, Titania twisted to smile. Yet, she did not speak. She hesitated as though questioning herself. As though ensuring she was happy with how the game was about to begin.

"John, take off your coat, waistcoat, and shirt."

It was a little early in the proceedings to think about making love, that was true, but John did not even consider disobeying. His fingers moved to his jacket, and it was lying on the floor before he had a chance to take a breath.

John swallowed as he allowed his shirt to fall to the floor. It was not cold in the private room, but there was something electric in the air between them now. The game was now afoot.

He was half-naked. There was a blindfold in her hands and a smile on her lips.

What in God's name could happen next?

"And are you going to tell me what happens next in this game?"

He had spoken as disinterestedly as possible, but there was certain breathiness that betrayed his excitement.

Titania had not looked away as he had undressed.

John did not shy away from her inspection. He was not arrogant, at least not knowingly so, and he knew he was a well-featured man—but it was a little strange to have a beautiful woman staring at him as she commanded him to undress.

Titania stepped forward.

"What are you—"

He could feel her warmth. He was captivated by her presence, by her scent, which he knew from somewhere but could not place. Lightness, lavender, a little rosemary oil. It was intoxicating.

Where had he smelled that before?

"Remember, this is a guessing game," came Titania's voice softly in his ear. John shivered and almost moaned as he felt her step away. "And this is how to play."

There was a scraping wooden sound—she had opened up another one of the drawers. *What was she about to remove from it?*

"I am going to touch you with items," came the Lyon Tamer's voice, soft and sweet. "And then you have to guess what they are."

John waited for her to continue and then found in the silence that she had finished.

"'Tis that simple?"

There was a laugh. It was followed by the sound of gentle footsteps—she was moving, and John turned his head wildly, utterly blind. Yet he followed her like a sunflower, dazzled by her brilliance.

By God, if only he could see her—but then, would he be driven this wild by desperate longing if he could?

"What happens if I guess correctly?"

"You win a point."

John shivered. *Christ alive, he wanted her.* He wanted her more than he had ever wanted anyone—more, and he felt a flicker of guilt at the thought than Miss Darby, and he had fallen head over heels in love with her.

"And...and if I guess wrong?" he croaked.

There was more laughter, but this time it came from a few feet away to his left.

"Well, then I win a point."

This was madness. Gentlemen did not just arrive at the Lyon's Den to be given a wife!

The rumors resurfaced in his mind. Certainly, it had happened—and by all accounts, they were happy marriages. *Why not?* It was no stranger when one thought about it than being introduced to a chit of a thing at a ball, barely speaking to her, and then offering for her hand.

Besides, he was no prisoner. He was not tied to the chair, the door was not locked, and if he wished to, he could remove the blindfold and simply step out of the room.

He could leave anytime he wanted, and yet he never would. Titania had bewitched him, tamed him with her voice, her elegance, her teasing smile.

And she knew him. She *knew him.* Better than anyone. The idea of marrying Titania, of having a wife who was that perfect mixture of beauty, intelligence, wit, and wildness in the bedchamber...

"And how long do we play for?" he found himself asking.

"First to six," came Titania's voice from the other side of the room.

"Sex?"

She laughed again. "Only if you are very lucky."

John could not help but moan at these words. *By God, she was a harlot—better, for it appeared she was going to follow through on these half-whispered promises.* Losing himself to her, loving her, was all he wanted in the world in this moment.

"You really are a temptress."

The words were out before he could stop them, but he was certain she would not be offended by the suggestion.

Though he could see nothing, he could almost imagine the wry smile she was giving him. "Yes, I am. And I am all yours if you are able to win me, John."

Something hot twisted in his lower stomach to hear his name on her lips. She could do whatever she wanted with him, anything at all, and she knew it.

"In that case," he breathed, "I am ready to begin."

The instant the words were out of his mouth, something touched him on the shoulder. He jerked away instinctively, but it was not painful. It was something soft.

"A feather," John said confidently.

"Very good," murmured Titania from behind him.

Christ, she was so close. If he were badly behaved, he could reach out and touch her—pull her into his arms, into his lap, and kiss her so hard she would beg to have him.

"That is a point to you," came her voice, interrupting his thoughts.

Silence fell in the room, and then something colder touched him, teasing down his shoulder blade. John took a deep breath and closed his eyes to concentrate—not that it would matter.

It was something...something wooden? Something small.

"A...a pencil?"

Titania laughed softly. "Well done, John. I am impressed."

Before he had a moment to feel the pleasure of her praise, something touched his arm. It was strange; at once hard, and then soft. Some part of it rustled. It sounded like—

"A book," John said quietly, his heart thundering. He had never been more vulnerable, sitting here with no sight as a stranger touched him with objects he could not see.

It was hedonistic and drove him wilder than he had ever been before. *Bloody hell, he wanted to sink himself into her and—*

"You are very good at this game," whispered Titania. She was so close to him, and she must be kneeling at his side as she murmured into his ear. "Very good. Are you desperate to win me?"

John swallowed. "More desperate than I thought."

The words were true. *Three points.* That meant he was halfway to winning her—and he knew what he would do as soon as they were married. Perhaps every day they were married.

Tear off those clothes, and—

"Christ," he moaned.

It had not been his thoughts that had prompted such a blasphemy. It was what she had touched him with. If he was not very much mistaken, Titania was gently moving her finger across his chest.

John twisted in his seat, leaning into her touch. It was so brief and yet sent shock waves through him, rocking him to his very core.

"You," he murmured.

There was that delicate laugh again. "I am not sure whether that is an exact guess, John, do you? What part of me?"

"Finger," John managed to say as the sensation of her fingertip moved to the very top of his breeches and then disappeared altogether.

"Very good."

"Christ and all his saints," John muttered, leaning back in his chair, attempting to catch his breath.

She was going to kill him if he did not bed her soon. *How could he stay in control of himself?*

Titania had not touched him with something new. She had placed herself in his lap—where his hands had been resting. And now his hands were touching…she was leaning into his chest.

He wondered whether he would ever be as close to Heaven before he died as he was right now. Titania, his Lyon Tamer, the woman who would win him for her husband if she won this game…

She was not wearing any underclothes. His hands were suddenly full of soft, warm flesh.

"Titania," he managed to groan. "I want…bloody hell…"

John tightened his fingers around her buttocks and felt pleasure rocket through him that he had never known. Her weight was comforting, her scent overwhelming, and he was going to...*if she were not careful, she would lose any chance to take him to that bed.*

"I-I am not sure I can play anymore," John moaned.

Her weight tilted, and there was a gentle laugh in his ear. "Dear me, John, giving up so soon? Does this mean you forfeit?"

CHAPTER SIX

IT WAS ALL too easy to lose herself in the sensations threatening to overwhelm her—and why shouldn't she let them? After waiting so long, after wanting him so much, why shouldn't Rebecca allow her fantasy to finally become a reality?

The feel of John's hands was wonderful. It made her lose all reason.

His hands on her bottom, her hands on his chest as she leaned on him, allowing her bosom to brush against his chest—oh God, it was heavenly, it was what life was intended for. It was what her life should have been for the last year at least!

Why had she not done this before?

"Oh, Titania," John moaned, still blindfolded.

Rebecca had to bite her lip to prevent herself from telling him precisely who she was. She wanted to hear her real name on his lips, but not yet. This was wild, wanton, wonderful, and she did not want it to end quickly.

Once she lost herself to him, once her innocence was gone…

Once, in short, they were more tied to each other than any other two people could be, when there was no going back, she could reveal herself to him.

"John…" she murmured.

She had promised herself she would not be too vulnerable, not open herself to him before he knew—but how could she restrain herself?

"Well, I am no fool, and I know what is likely to occur here. And I have not…I have never…not before. Not with anyone."

He was just as innocent as she was. Rebecca's heart swelled with joy at the thought they would experience this newness together, share it as equals—it was more than she could ever have hoped for.

It was time to get her way.

"I said," Rebecca murmured, attempting to keep her voice level, "does this mean you forfeit?"

"I-I do forfeit," John moaned, seemingly unable to stop stroking her bottom.

"How about having the rest of me?"

Rebecca could hardly believe she had said those words. She had to offer herself to him, knowing he needed to make the choice. She could not just make this part of the game; that would taint it, somehow. *He needed to want her.*

"Wh-What?" John was panting, and Rebecca could feel his racing heartbeat beneath her fingertips, still resting on his chest. "The…the rest of you."

It was not a question. He knew precisely what she was suggesting, and as Rebecca removed her hands from his chest to reach up to the ties on her mask, she examined his face.

He did not look confused. She knew what she meant. So, as she dropped her mask to the floor and felt her heart rate quicken, *why was he hesitating?*

John was still blindfolded; he could not see her. *Perhaps that was it.* But was she brave enough to show him the truth?

"I want you."

Rebecca blinked. Had he really said… "I beg your pardon?"

A sardonic smile tilted John's lips. "You heard me. I want you, Titania, Lyon Tamer, whoever you are. You are in control. Take me."

Rebecca stared, unsure whether she could move. There was no possibility he could tell who she was, not with that blindfold on. As long as she was careful—she had been delicate in her description of herself, and there was nothing about her, surely, that could identify her by touch?

Her cheeks colored as John's fingers moved to her hips, and he moaned again. *No, they had never been this intimate when she was Miss Rebecca Darby. Why not, now she was the Lyon Tamer?*

Rebecca leaned forward, closed her eyes, and kissed John on the lips.

They had kissed before. This was not new territory for them, although he did not know it, and yet it was utterly different. The instant her lips touched his, her whole body seemed to spark to life.

Had she been sleepwalking through life until this moment? That was what it felt like; the kiss heated her, changed her, made her cling to him as though the world would end if she even considered letting go.

And John responded in turn. His hands clung onto her lower back, pulling her as close as was possible, desperate, eager—*hungry.*

Rebecca felt the kiss change. John's tongue was teasing her lips, and she welcomed him in, hungry for more of a connection. She moaned in his mouth as his tongue teased her, ravishing it for all pleasure.

Eventually—she could not tell how long they were kissing there on the chair—Rebecca pulled away.

"No," he breathed. "Come back here."

"No," Rebecca teased, her breathing short. "Not here. The bed?"

This time there was no hesitation. John nodded, releasing her from his grip as his fingers moved toward his blindfold.

"No!"

His hands paused at the sound of her urgent voice.

"You have to keep it on," said Rebecca slowly.

This, she was certain of. Until she had entirely seduced him, until they were one, she could not be entirely sure John would marry her. And he had to marry her, for that was the whole point of this game.

She glanced at the bed. *Well, the primary point.*

Rebecca rose to her feet and reached out to take John by the hand. He rose willingly, tall and masculine as only John was. It took but seconds to lead him to the bed.

"Lie down," she whispered.

And this was where the plan ended, Rebecca thought ruefully as she stood by the bed and looked down. For all of Mrs. Dove-Lyon's clever ideas, she had not provided any expertise for this step.

It did not matter. For the first time in her life, she was filled with the certainty that whatever she did would be right.

"You may be blindfolded," Rebecca whispered, "but that does not mean you cannot enjoy me undressing."

John turned toward the sound of her voice. "What do you—"

"I am slowly untying the ribbons of my bodice," said Rebecca quietly. "My...my fingers are warm against my skin."

The effect was instantaneous. John moaned as his body twitched.

"Now the ribbons have fallen to the floor, and the only thing holding up my gown are my fingers," she whispered.

"Christ alive, Titania," John groaned, pulling at his breeches to remove them.

As they fell to the floor, Rebecca could not take her eyes away from... *Well.* She had known the theory, of course.

"I...I am pulling down my gown," she continued.

John, now utterly naked, moved to the edge of the bed and reached out for her. "Come here."

Rebecca laughed, stepping aside from his questing fingers. "Not yet—remember, you forfeited the game, John. That means you do what I say."

But they were naked together. She was about to experience every-thing that she had ever dreamed of, and then they would be married and be happy forever.

IF HE WEREN'T careful, John knew he was going to come just thinking about the woman who was standing mere feet from him.

Bloody hell, he was in deep here—a real expert, a woman who could drive him wild just by the sound of her voice!

God knew what other delights she was keeping from him.

John reached out again in the darkness, and there was that laugh again. *Damn and blast it, she was avoiding his fingertips, and that was only driving him closer to the edge!*

This Lyon Tamer felt intimately known to him, and yet that could not be. No woman in his acquaintance would ever act in this way!

Play a game with a blindfold? Tease him with her finger, offer herself to him on his lap?

John shivered. No, ladies of good reputation did not do such things. When she was his wife, he would ensure she was given a little training on how to behave like a lady—at least, in public.

She could behave exactly like this when they were alone.

"You wanton, wild thing," he said aloud with a groan. "God, I want you here in my arms, damnit!"

Fingertips across his chest—John grasped for her, but she slipped from his reach, and he moaned with disappointment at the scant touch he had enjoyed.

This was the sort of woman he wanted—someone who was not fazed by his charm, good looks, and title.

The Lyon Tamer leaned closer and whispered, "All in good time."

A jolt went through John. As she grew closer, that scent filled his mind again, and it reminded him of…

But it wasn't her. Miss Rebecca Darby would never be so brave, so foolish as to risk her reputation by coming to an establishment like the Lyon's Den.

The thought of her caused a flicker of guilt through John's heart. She was the one he had fallen in love with—the first and only woman who had truly captured his heart. If only he had been braver. If only he had spoken out when he had had the chance.

John closed his eyes and remembered the sensations of Titania's bottom in his palms, and tried not to explode. Miss Darby would never do anything like this. What he wanted was a mixture of both. The laughter, joy, beauty of Miss Darby, and the elegance and wild sensuality of this woman.

"Come here, damn you, I want you," he said aloud, reaching out his hands.

John shivered. "Where are you?"

Fingers that seemed nervous touched his shoulder. "Here, John."

Some of the bravado seemed to have left his Titania. *Was she…was it too much to suppose that she was nervous?*

It did not make sense. She had chosen to play this particular game with him, true—but surely Mrs. Dove-Lyon's ladies have worked the tables on the gambling floor before? *She was not a virgin?*

John recalled the elegance of her walk, the beauty of her eyes, and moaned slightly under his breath. He was about to lose his innocence.

"Please," he whispered, unable to help himself. "I want you. Show me."

"Are you ready?"

Her voice was so close to him now that John did not have to guess. He could simply act. Reaching out, his fingers brushed past her breasts as he pulled her onto him.

"John!"

He could not see but heard the pleasure in her voice and reveled in the sensation of her upon him. Her weight was perfect, her breasts against his chest, her legs nestled in with his... It was as though they had been made for each other, as though he had come home.

"Christ, Titania, you feel..." John wasn't able to finish the sentence. He did not have words to describe these sorts of feelings—the way her breasts pulled up against him, the curve of her hips, the way she was pressed up against his manhood. "I want—"

He did not continue; he could not. She had understood him perfectly and was now kissing him as though her life depended on it. *And who knows, perhaps it did?*

He was lost in the wild sensations of passion, as her softness and her beauty became almost visible to him under his questing fingers, moving over her, exploring every part of her—he wanted to know all of her.

The thought that he would be doing this again, and again, as her husband and with the blindfold off was enough to push John over the edge. Still, he battled to keep control of his body—his body which had only seemed to come alive, for the first time in his life, as Titania touched him.

"Can I take the blindfold off, now?" He panted the question rather than asked it.

There was that subtle laugh again. *Had he ever heard it before, outside of the Lyon's Den?*

"No, John, I told you—because you forfeited the game, you have to do what I say, remember?"

John nodded, his lips once again captured by her. He wanted to see her desperately, but the blindfold did not ruin their encounter. In a way, it accelerated the excitement. It was nice not to be in control. The Lyon Tamer could take the lead.

And then she was gone. John gasped at the shock of her absence, sat up in the bed in a desperate attempt to find her again—and then cried out.

"God in his Heaven!"

Titania had not gone. She had moved.

He didn't need to see to kiss her. He wasn't aiming for her lips, after all—he was going to kiss every single inch of her.

After what felt like a wonderful lifetime of adoration, Titania turned him, so she was once again on top of him, this time straddling him.

"Are you ready?"

The phrase itself was innocent, but John knew what she meant.

"Yes. Tame me."

As soon as the tip of his manhood entered her, John cried out. There were no words; there could not be any words for this sensation, and he wondered how any man, once knowing this pleasure, this joy, this ecstasy, could ever live a day of his life without it.

He had to be careful, as she slowly lowered herself onto him, not to explode into her straight away. She needed her pleasure, and he had to remember that. *He had to try to control himself.*

John bit his lip in concentration. The intensity was overwhelming, but he would be master of himself. *He would not be a disappointment for her.*

"Oh, John, you feel…"

Rebecca's words did not precisely make sense to him, but that did not matter. Before he could say anything, she was rocking up and down against him, and John grasped at her hips, as though he would fall off the face of the earth if he did not.

"Yes, yes," he moaned. "More, yes!"

"Oh, John, John, John…" she whimpered.

It was as though all the days of his life had been leading up to this, and all he could do was cling on and enjoy the ride.

But there was something building, building inside of him, and if he was not careful…

"Titania, I am going to—I can't stop—"

"John!" She shuddered against him, her whole body rocking with the pleasure crest she was riding.

Finally. John took her pleasure as permission, and then he was shooting into her, rocking against her, and he could see stars against the blindfold as the Lyon Tamer, the woman he would spend the rest of his life with, fell against him.

John held her in his arms as they both gasped for breath. *He never wanted to be tamed by anyone else.*

CHAPTER SEVEN

WRAPPED IN HIS arms, unsure how to breathe, Rebecca tried to collect herself and utterly failed.

Breathing, yes. She needed to do that. If she didn't, she would expire and never again experience the absolute delight of being one with John.

John. She tilted her head to look at him. He looked just as out of breath as she after their lovemaking. Was it possible that he, too, was wondering why he had waited this long in his life to find her?

Rebecca forced down the feeling. *John had not found her.* He had no idea who she was!

He was hers now. No matter what happened, she would always belong to him. The idea she could ever feel affection for any other gentleman, it was ludicrous! She adored him, and now they had shared this together...

"Christ alive," he breathed. "That was...it was..."

Rebecca laughed gently. "Yes, that was just what I was thinking."

He did not need to know just how nervous she was, after all. She did not want him to know she was already doubting him.

"Now then, my Titania, my Lyon Tamer," John said with a smile.

"I cannot express how much I want to see you, see all of you, especially after that… Can I take my blindfold off yet?"

Rebecca hesitated. "No."

What made her stop? She could not extend this indefinitely; at some point, John would have to remove the blindfold and see the lady who had taken his innocence and given hers.

But not yet. She wanted to stay unknown for just a few more minutes.

"I have never experienced anything like that," John said quietly, breaking the silence.

Rebecca laughed softly. "Neither have I."

She felt foolish as soon as the words were out of her mouth, but John laughed. "You are on the hunt for a husband, then? It looks like I was the lucky winner."

She stroked his chest. "I was on the hunt for you."

John's head turned toward her. "Me?"

Rebecca nodded, and then realizing he could not see her, said, "Yes, you. I knew…well, that you would not necessarily be impressed by all the normal rules of courting. I knew I had to tame you in a different way than you expected."

John laughed. "You certainly did!"

She felt his laugh as well as heard it, rocking through her body, their bodies, as they clung to each other.

"I had hoped…well," she said, swallowing. She had to start speaking truths, or she would never remove his blindfold. "I think I got more than I bargained for!"

THE BLINDFOLD WAS starting to irritate John, but he still obeyed.

She was impressive. Titania was elegant, feminine, and yet power-ful.

He felt...how did he feel with her in his arms?

As though he had beaten every man in the world to win her heart. As though she was a great prize for something he had done—though God knew what he could possibly have done to win her.

It was a rather heady thought. She had known him well...

"You like opera, but you do not love it. You prefer concerts—Mozart, mainly. You adore cards, but you are not very good. Yet you never cheat."

But more than that, she had desired him so much that she had spoken to Mrs. Dove-Lyon and concocted some wild sort of game to win him.

He was here only because a woman wanted him.

John racked his brains, running through all the ladies in his acquaintance, of which they were many. Some were bold, and many were clever, and almost all beautiful.

None of them would surely do this—would they?

"You know me."

There was a shift of the weight on his chest, and then, "Yes, I think I have made that rather obvious."

John smiled. "No, I mean...you know who I am, but you also know me. The opera, concerts, all those other things...and it is almost as though you know how I want to be touched, how I want to be loved."

The words sounded strange on his lips, but he had to say them. *He had to ask.*

"But that would mean...it would suggest, at the very least, that we have met, several times. Tell me. Tell me your name."

Silence. Nothing but the beating of his heart and the warmth of her skin.

And then she spoke—hesitantly at first, but with a little strength growing with each passing syllable. "I thought you would have guessed by now. I thought you would know me by my voice."

John desperately wracked his mind, his memory, but there were so many young ladies in society.

She knew him. He knew her.

John almost shook his head with self-disgust. *That was the best he could manage?*

"I do apologize," he said quietly, and he meant it. "I cannot think of who you could be, and I am ashamed to admit it. I must have been walking around with my eyes half-closed."

A movement—she was shifting in his arms, and John instinctively tightened his grip, as though afraid he would lose her.

"Yes, you were, that is a very apt description," came her quiet voice. "Time and time again, I thought you would notice me, but then...you always had eyes for others. Though I did always enjoy our time together."

Damn and blast, he had spent time with her? John's feelings of guilt increased. What sort of cad was he that he had utterly ignored what was the perfect woman for him?

"If I had known, really known you, when I met you in the world, I am sure I would have offered for you," said John quietly. "I swear it. You have no reason to believe me, I suppose, but—"

"I believe everything you say." There was only truth and a certain amount of innocence in her tones.

John stroked her arm gently, reveling in her warmth. "So...can I take my blindfold off now? Please?"

The pause was enough evidence of her hesitation, and then she said, "You remember the rules, I am sure, John. You lost the game—"

"Forfeited the game!" John protested.

There was a gentle laugh. "Forfeited, but still. You did not win. That means you must do what I want."

John grinned. "I thought that was the lovemaking."

Her fingers were gently tracing his collarbones now, and John gloried in her touch. *So gentle. So sensual.*

"That is what happened, but I want something different. I want you to marry me."

John swallowed. He had known it, known this was coming, and for some reason, he felt no qualms about agreeing to her request.

Was he foolish to make this commitment to a woman he had not really seen? He had spent—what, minutes in her presence without the blindfold? *How could he agree to marry a woman he barely knew?*

His wandering fingers moved down her arm to her hip, cupping her buttocks. Well, he did know her very well in some ways, far better than some gentlemen knew their wives before they were strolling up the aisle.

After all, was this not the perfect opportunity? He had been too shy to propose matrimony to a woman who had captured his heart, so what made him think he would ever be successful? *Was this not perfect, a woman offering herself to him?*

This was wild, ridiculous, and his gut told him he would not have it any other way.

"I will."

The words were croaked more than spoken, and he was not surprised when Titania asked the question.

"You will? You will marry me?"

John nodded. "I will marry you."

Soft and gentle hands moved to his face, fingers untying the knot in the blindfold which was, finally, removed.

John blinked in the sudden brightness, and as his eyes adjusted to the light, he saw lying beside him in the bed…*Rebecca Darby.*

CHAPTER EIGHT

H IS EXPRESSION FELL, and his mouth dropped open.
It was like death. It was torture. It was all she had hoped to avoid and more, because now, instead of *imagining* the very worst ending to her rebellious time at the Lyon's Den, she was now forced to look at it with her own eyes.

Panic rushed through her veins as John's disappointment and confusion became stronger, gaping as though he had never seen a woman before.

What a mistake she had made. What a fool she was! Rebecca blinked away the tears appearing in the corners of her eyes. She should never have even considered such a foolish thing—she was an idiot to think she could just turn up at the Lyon's Den and make John love her.

Her plan had been described by Mrs. Dove-Lyon as foolproof, but she was the fool. What had her greatest fear been? That John would reject her, that he would not marry her.

Why else make him promise to marry her before he took the dammed blindfold off?

But despite her careful planning, despite her making him say it…

"I will marry you."

"M-Miss Darby!"

Rebecca closed her eyes at John's words. She could not bear it. It was intolerable to hear his disappointment and confusion.

"Yes, I am Miss Darby," she said aloud, a little defensively.

Well, she had gone against her instincts in an attempt to win him, and she had failed. Now it was time to face the consequences.

"Rebecca Darby," John said blankly.

Was that all he could say? Rebecca found her bruised heart growing angry and tried to calm it. There was no point in blaming the poor man for her mistakes. If she had just acted as a young lady, then she would not be in this mess.

And what had Mrs. Dove-Lyon said?

"Make sure you are absolutely sure of him—no, do not misunderstand me, Miss, absolutely sure of him. That means getting his promise, on his word of honor, and only then can you even consider revealing yourself to him. Men are tricky beasts, Miss Darby, and they are not to be trusted until they are to be trusted."

Rebecca moved further away from John in the bed—in the bed where they had... *No, she must not think about that.* She had been sure that John would marry her. Had he not said that?

"I will marry you."

"I cannot believe it is you," said John weakly. He was sitting up now, still utterly naked.

Rebecca attempted not to look at his...well, at all of him. When she did, she saw everything she had always wanted in a husband.

"I-I would never have guessed—" John began.

Rebecca laughed bitterly. "Yes, no one believes that silly Miss Darby could be elegant, or womanly, or...or..."

Betrayal rushed through her heart. She had thought he would fight for her—fight against his expectations of her—and see her for the woman she was. *Had she not just given him proof that she could be the wife he wanted?*

But the last hour or so had done nothing to make her more of a wife in his eyes than the last year. Even after making love to her, John did not believe she was worthy of him.

"No, 'tis not that," said John hastily. "It is more…well, you are not normally…you were always…"

His voice trailed away as his gaze dropped to his hands, seemingly unable to look at her.

And it was that which pushed her over the edge. She did not have to put up with this. She had done her best, and that was not good enough.

Time to leave.

"I should have known this was a mistake," she said quietly, moving off the bed and stepping toward the ridiculous gown Mrs. Dove-Lyon had insisted she wear. "I will be gone in but a moment, and then you can—"

"Gone?" repeated John as though he had been hit over the head. "What do you mean, gone?"

"Gone," said Rebecca shortly. She did not want to spend another minute in this room, the room where she had gambled so much and lost. She had to get as far away from John as possible.

She could never see him again. She would have to trust that he would never reveal the truth of their encounter to the world—more, she would have to pray that, in her foolishness, she had not just created a child.

THE RUSH OF emotions crowding John's thoughts prevented him from understanding what was happening before him.

Rebecca Darby!

It could not be. His eyes must be deceiving him—it was only because Miss Darby was always so much on his mind that he was seeing her before him.

And yet, no matter how much he blinked, Miss Darby had not disappeared.

He was the world's biggest fool. *Miss Darby!* The woman had been the one person to steal his heart, even if he had never admitted it to her, and yet she was miles away from the confident, sensual being who had teased him...

John needed to do something. He needed to say something, but his breathing was as uncontrolled as his thoughts.

"Wait, Rebecca—Miss Darby—wait!"

She ignored him. John swallowed, his mind still racing.

Was he...he had agreed to marry Miss Darby!

It was like all his dreams had come together and provided him with a solution he could never have conspired to create.

And yet, she seemed so upset, so confused by his shock. *What was so surprising about it?* After the chattering Miss Darby he had thought he knew so well, was he not to be surprised that the Titania who had teased him with her gentle touches and silences could be the same person?

A headache was starting to throb in his temple, but John pushed aside the pain. *Marrying Miss Darby.* It was a heady thought, one that gave him as much joy as the confusion of her real identity.

If their married life could be full of that lovemaking...

"Miss Darby—Rebecca," he added hastily. It did not seem right, somehow, to speak in such a formal way. "Please, wait, I want to talk to you."

"There is nothing to talk about," Rebecca said hurriedly, pulling her gown above her breasts. "I should never have come here. I should never have hoped that..."

Her agony was evident, but why? He had said nothing, done nothing wrong?

"Why *did* you come here? Plan this?"

His curiosity got the better of him, and John wondered whether he had crossed some invisible line, offending her.

But he had to ask; he had to know.

"'Tis none of your business," Rebecca said shortly, dropping her gaze.

John's defensiveness sparked. "I think it is!"

She was now focused on attempting to tie the myriads of ribbons down the sides of her bodice, but her fingers scrabbled against them and did not manage to tie a single one.

"I…I had heard. You must have heard, too, about the Lyon's Den," was what she murmured.

She felt betrayed by him. Had he not reacted with the right amount of enthusiasm when she had revealed herself to him? *Was he supposed to have jumped for joy?*

John swallowed. *Perhaps he should have done.* If he were brave, he would have admitted, right there and then, that he had fallen in love with her over a year ago and had never known how to…

Now, with that opportunity before him, with Rebecca Darby naked in a bed with him…

He had panicked. *Was that so wrong?*

"Mrs. Dove-Lyon said she would help me," said Rebecca quietly, her hands now falling to her sides.

John nodded mutely, still not trusting his voice. This entire evening, then—the invitation, the game, Rebecca Darby—it was all created by her to win him, to gain his promise to marry her.

Marry her. He smiled. Marriage to Rebecca Darby was going to be far more exciting than he ever thought. *Perhaps they could play that game again; perhaps next time—*

"And so here I am," Rebecca said bitterly. "And you did not know me at all."

John opened his mouth but then closed it again. *What was he supposed to say? Yes, I did not recognize you when you were masked, dressed in a gown more suitable to a whore than a lady, and then I was blindfolded?*

All those letters she had sent him, full of nonsense, not asking anything in particular, hinting at a wish to see him but nothing more.

It was difficult to believe the hand which had penned such messages was the same hand to touch him as he sat blindfolded on the chair.

Only now did he see she had wanted him to propose to her. Wanted it, wanted *him* so much that she had invited him to the Lyon's Den.

"My God, those letters—you wished to marry me," John said aloud without a second thought. "Why did you not say something before?"

CHAPTER NINE

"MY GOD, THOSE *letters—you wished to marry me. Why did you not say something before?*"

The words echoed around the room as Rebecca's mouth fell open. *Did he say…did John say what she thought she said?*

And he was laughing. Her personal agonies over the last year, the feelings of rejection, the terror he may marry another, the pain when she saw him flirting with other ladies, the knowledge she would never be happy unless she was with him…none of that mattered to him.

John was not the gentleman she had thought he was. Rebecca could not help but stare as he laughed at her predicament and distress.

But she was not just Miss Darby, not anymore. She was Titania here. The place seeped bravery into her pores just when she needed it, though in a way, it had always been there, deep inside her. She had just never realized it.

She was going to say the things she had always wanted to say. She was going to speak the truth.

"You do not understand, do you?" Her voice was quiet, controlled, and it wiped the smile from John's face immediately.

"Understand?" he repeated. "I think I understand far better than I did before, at any rate. You love me, you wished to marry me, and that is why we are here. What I can't understand is why you never said anything before today! Why, there were so many times we—"

"So that is a no, you do not understand," cut in Rebecca with a wry smile. "Well, at least you tried, I suppose."

John frowned, obviously utterly at sea.

Rebecca sighed. All the education that England could give him, yet there was still so much he did not comprehend.

"Ladies cannot simply decide they wish to marry someone and propose to them—the very idea!" she said cuttingly. "Have you ever stepped a foot outside of your own experience, John, and imagined what it is like to have no agency, no control, no direction in one's life other than that which a man gives you? Father, brother, husband…ladies have no choice in their lives. Not out there."

It was wonderful to speak so plainly, and Rebecca felt a rush of euphoria flow through her. She should have done this years ago.

"That is not exactly true," said John hastily. "I know plenty of ladies who—Lady Romeril, for example…"

His voice trailed away as Rebecca laughed dryly. "Dear God, you cannot intend to give her as an example? John, the woman is near eighty! A wealthy widow who has age on her side can certainly do what she wants, but me? No. No, I waited for you, and you did nothing."

It was not intended as an accusation, but it hung in the air like one, and she saw John bristle.

"You gave me no indication—"

"I sent you letters! Far beyond what was expected of a young lady, I may add, and if my father had ever discovered I had…" Rebecca swallowed. *If her father ever discovered she had ever heard of the Lyon's Den, let alone step foot inside it…* "I gave you all the hints I could, as a lady."

But John was shaking his head. *Had he not listened to her, had he not understood?*

"How was I supposed to know from those letters that your affections for me were so...so progressed?"

It was Rebecca's turn to hesitate. "I-I...You are the Lion of the Lennoxes! I thought you would be able to see through the words on the page, understand what I was trying to say."

John had risen now and was shaking his head as he started to pace around the room. "You think I am some sort of mind reader? You think I can translate meaningless phrases about attending the opera to...to a proposal?"

Rebecca could feel herself getting hot. This was not the time to lose her temper. She needed to stay calm so she could explain to John precisely why he was in the wrong.

"You know how you gained your nickname?" she said, moving to sit in the armchair near the bed. "The Lion of the Lennoxes?"

"No."

Rebecca smiled. "Because of the way you gather the ladies around you, you must have noticed."

He had stopped his pacing and was now leaning against the wall. "Well? What of it? 'Tis hardly my fault if ladies wish to spend some time with me. I have never encouraged them, never promised things I could not—"

"The last time," Rebecca repeated, and there was sadness in her tones. "Damnit, John, why aren't you listening to me? I never got a proper look in again. How could I-I impress you, shy as I was, when you were so surrounded?"

He did not reply to this. Rebecca's heart was fluttering painfully.

"You only invited me to the opera with Lady Charlotte because I was there before you, and you felt embarrassed. I can see that now," she said simply. "God, I was so foolish. Here I was, convinced you were falling in love with me, and you did not even recognize me this evening."

Sadness was threatening to overwhelm her, but there was still a little fury, too, and that was the emotion she held on to.

Fury would help her continue to speak. Righteous anger, that's what it was. She needed to say this, needed to explain. Because without this moment, she would always wonder, always question herself, question him.

Rebecca took a deep breath to continue, but John cut across her.

"I think you are being unfair," he said curtly. "Damnit, Miss Darby—Rebecca, I asked you to that opera because I wanted you to come! I thought you pretty, and I knew nothing of you, and I thought to find out more!"

Something akin to hope sparked in her mind, but Rebecca pushed it away. She could not allow herself to get overwhelmed by John's clever words. She had fallen for these tricks before.

"But you never considered me a serious prospect, did you?"

John took a step toward her. "I had not considered matrimony to any—"

Rebecca laughed. "Oh, John, I do want to believe you, but I just cannot! I saw the way you looked at the other ladies around us at that card party we attended together. It is always the beautiful ones, the witty ones, who marry! Not...not the shy ones."

John. Even looking at him now, she found herself utterly besotted with him. Love was in her bones, and she would never rid herself of him.

Even if she wanted to, John was a part of her, especially now. But he had to understand.

"You—you are shy?"

Rebecca did not know why John looked so astonished. "Why do you think I chatter away, fill the awkward silences, struggle to allow anyone to get in edgeways?"

Why did she have to prostrate herself at John's feet, remind him of all her faults? She was supposed to be angry with him!

"I talk when I am nervous, and no one wants to hear that. They just get bored of me, I can see it in their eyes. I am no fool," said Rebecca, hating her mouth for running away but unable to stop it.

"I was never bored with you, Rebecca."

John's voice was soft, and he had taken another step toward her. She could hardly look at him. Her love was overwhelming, and she knew if she were not careful, she would move to be crushed in his arms, leaving all the pain and questioning behind.

But she couldn't. There had been no declarations of love from John, nothing like that. All she wanted was John to love her. It did not have to be a perfect love—goodness knows, no one was perfect. But something. Some affection.

"Look, I made a promise to you," said John quickly, his voice low. "And I intend to keep it. I will marry you."

The temptation to merely accept, to nod, to move forward and kiss him and cry she had finally achieved her aim, swept over Rebecca.

But she couldn't.

"No."

John frowned. "What do you mean, no? You love me, don't you?"

Rebecca did not deign to respond to such a question. "I...I care about you, John, but you never noticed me. You honor this promise in an attempt to make yourself feel better, for your sense of honor, and that is not the sort of marriage I—"

"That is not what I am—"

"You never really noticed me," she said simply. "Even here, you did not recognize me, not after more than a year of... No, I will not marry you."

"Damnit, Rebecca, this is what you wanted—I am giving you what you wanted!" John looked a little deranged, his hair all over the place, one hand to his temple as he stared. "This was your idea, all of it!"

"I know," said Rebecca sadly. "And in a way, 'tis freeing to finally have this out. All these things I wanted to say but never had the courage to. Well, I have the courage now."

John resumed his pacing, evidently unable to face her any longer, and Rebecca found herself sagging in the chair. The concentration she was forced to maintain so close to him…it was almost overwhelming.

But she would not be overwhelmed. *She was the Lyon Tamer.*

"I wanted to tame you, and you know…I think I have failed," Rebecca said quietly as she rose. "I thought if you simply experienced me in a different way, you would…but I was wrong."

It was time to leave. She could not stay here a moment longer, not with John pacing around like a caged lion, still half undressed. Her self-control could not hold forever, and if he pulled her into his arms and kissed her, she would certainly make promises that she would not be able to keep outside of the Lyon's Den.

The Lyon's Den. She had thought everything could be solved here, like some sort of perfect world.

But a visit to the Lyon's Den was not a miracle. Not all problems could be solved by a visit—it had just made everything worse.

Rebecca grabbed her mask, which she had left on the desk by the door. Now John knew her wantonness, knew what she was willing to do to win him, now there was a chance there would be a child, and he knew she was no longer innocent…

She took a deep breath as she tried to calm her frantic mind. *She needed to stay composed.* Nothing could be gained by focusing on all the disasters of the evening.

She at least knew now where she stood with John, and that was not at the altar.

After sharing everything with him, all of herself, her fears, the truth of her shyness, her body…it wasn't enough. Not to tempt him to make a genuine offer.

He did not want her. He did not love her. Naught but honor forced him to keep to his promise—a promise she had exacted without him even knowing her name.

"Where you are—wait!"

John had evidently realized her intentions, but Rebecca could not wait. Not a single minute more could be spent in his company, for the tears she had forced away when she had seen his disappointment in her true identity were threatening to return.

She did not wish to cry in front of him. Not even if the pain of losing him, irrevocably and forever, cut into her stomach like a knife.

Staying here was impossible.

"Goodbye, John," said Rebecca without looking around. The door was shut behind his reply.

The gambling floor was unbearably loud after the relative silence of the room.

No, she could not think of him. She must not.

Walking away quickly, Rebecca did not even look where she was going. It did not matter. She had to put as much distance between her and that room as possible, in case—

"Ah, I wondered when you would be reappearing." Mrs. Dove-Lyon appeared before her, a cigar in her hand. "Well?"

A blush tinged Rebecca's cheeks. She had not expected to see anyone or have to talk to anyone after making love for the first time. It had been a private moment, a monumental shift in her own body, and all she wished to do was return home.

But it was her establishment. Mrs. Dove-Lyon probably had some sort of right to know what had occurred, in broad terms.

Mrs. Dove-Lyon did not speak again, merely raising an eyebrow.

Rebecca shook her head. Words were not sufficient to explain the depths of misery she was feeling, and saying the words aloud would make them final. *It was too painful.*

"He will not marry you? Come, let us away to my private sitting room—and put that mask on, if you do not wish to be identified."

Rebecca hastened with the mask, tying it around her as they walked toward a door. Mrs. Dove-Lyon opened it, and Rebecca stepped through.

The sitting room was rather like an older lady's parlor: cozy, but with fashions from several years ago in the furnishings and paintings. The silence was welcome after the raucous noise of the gambling floor.

"Sit," ordered Mrs. Dove-Lyon, pointing to an armchair by the little grate, taking a seat herself.

Rebecca obeyed and sighed. "He...he said he would after I removed my mask."

Mrs. Dove-Lyon waited for the rest of her sentence. "Then I do not understand what the problem is, Titania."

Titania. It was a foolish name, and Rebecca wished she had thought more about it before she had started this ridiculous charade.

Titania. She started Shakespeare's play in an argument with her husband, Oberon, and then spent most of it in love with an ass.

Perhaps it was only right she be given such a name. What a shame she was not going to experience Titania's happy ending.

"I could not bear the disappointment on his face when he saw who I was," said Rebecca quietly. "That is not how I want to get married—I want my husband to be wildly, passionately in love with me. I want marriage to me to be the best thing that has ever happened in his life. Not a consolation prize at the end of a game."

The bitterness in her voice was unlike her, but perhaps it would be now she had known real disappointment. After all, she only spoke the truth.

She should have known. Young ladies like herself did not get happily ever afters.

Mrs. Dove-Lyon, however, did not seem moved by Rebecca's plight. She shrugged.

"Some marriages of convenience or agreement are the best, in my experience."

Rebecca stared at the older lady. She knew very little about Mrs. Dove-Lyon, only what she had heard through the rumor mill, and most of that was not very detailed. That she was married herself was not even certain. Plenty of older ladies took on the moniker Mrs. as a form of respectability.

But if she had been married, and it had been a marriage of convenience, had she just offended her host?

Well, if she had, there was nothing she could do about that now.

"I could not bear that," Rebecca said quietly. "It...it is not for me."

Mrs. Dove-Lyon examined her for a moment and then sighed. "Well, the choice is yours, I am sure, but I worry you may come to regret it."

Rising to her feet, she offered her hand. "And now our time together is at an end. Give the mask to Helena on your way out. She is guarding the ladies' entry tonight."

Rebecca took her hand. "Thank you for everything. It did not end as I had hoped, but still, at least I know."

The woman nodded, and Rebecca turned toward the door. This was it. This was the last time she would be in the Lyon's Den, and she would never again have the chance to...

Tears finally poured down her cheeks. It was all over. She would not be John Lennox's wife.

CHAPTER TEN

ANOTHER DAY. ANOTHER breakfast. John looked across the table without seeing, unable to comprehend that his world had changed as much as it had.

Just a few days ago, this was just a breakfast table. Now it was the place he had been sitting when he had received the invitation to the Lyon's Den. His invitation from Miss Darby.

Rebecca.

He swallowed. The emptiness in his stomach was unlike anything he had ever known. Unsated by food, there was nothing on the table likely to fill the aching pain inside.

Besides, the world had lost its color.

John's chest tightened painfully, so suddenly that he clapped a hand to his chest as though that would remove the agony. The pain always resurfaced whenever his thoughts drifted to Rebecca. Whatever emotion this was, it was painful. *Love?*

What did it matter?

Rebecca had fitted him perfectly, in every way. The woman he had loved—a love that now, all too late, had only grown the more he had discovered about her.

And she loved him.

True, Rebecca had not said so in quite so many words, but surely that was why she had planned such a scheme, was it not? They had loved each other in their own ways, without the other knowing the depth of their passion, and it had all come together perfectly—*perfectly, that was, until it all fell apart…*

John sighed, picking up his teacup and taking a sip of his now cold tea. It all could have occurred a million years ago, and yet it had happened just a few hours before.

Sleep had eluded him, and his mind was clouded with the knowledge that Rebecca Darby believed the absolute worst of him.

He had chased after her, of course. His first instinct, once he had managed to get his shirt, waistcoat, and jacket on, was to fling open the door and stride onto the gambling floor to find her.

But she was gone. He had asked some of the ladies, naturally, but none of them had ever heard of a Titania.

John shook his head. *Of course, they had not.* They would never reveal details of a woman who had attended the Lyon's Den with the sole desire to gain his hand in marriage.

His bones ached, exhaustion seeping through them as though he had run a marathon. Returning home last night, he had been astonished to find it was only midnight.

Midnight? He had spent hours, days, perhaps weeks with Rebecca in the Lyon's Den, hadn't he?

John shivered at the memory of her sitting in his lap.

Miss Darby! How was he supposed to have guessed the sensual, bold woman in the mask who was quite evidently attempting to seduce him was the same chattering woman who had never known when to stop speaking?

"My, what a wonderful place! And to think, though my father and I have been in Bath a month, we have not been here! It does not seem quite right that we should come all this way for the Season and not even try some of its delights…"

That had been their first outing together and before the idea of courting had even entered his head. How could he marry the confident woman he had met in the Lyon's Den?

It simply did not make sense. They were two completely different women, Miss Rebecca Darby and the ravishing Titania, yet, they were the same.

"You never really noticed me. Even here, you did not recognize me, not after more than a year. No, I will not marry you."

John dropped his head into his hands.

"My word, still breakfasting!"

Startled, John looked up wildly and saw his brother, William, had strode into the room with his hat under his arm and a smile on his face.

"Yes," said John, a little more defensively than was probably called for. "What of it?"

His brother raised an eyebrow. "Nothing at all. Except...except your manservant here informs me you have been here for almost three hours without eating a thing. He wants to clear the room for luncheon."

John glanced at his pocket watch and saw with astonishment, it was nearer noon than eleven.

How was it possible that he had not noticed the time? Had he really sat here in silence, thinking about Rebecca, ignoring his food and the passage of the hours?

He sighed heavily.

"Oh dear," said William just as heavily, sitting opposite. "That does not sound good."

He allowed the two of them to drop into silence. John knew he was waiting for him to speak, but he would not.

He could not be trusted, not at the moment, not to pour out the whole sorry affair. He would not reveal Miss Darby to the world nor ruin her reputation. Even though he was probably the one who had ruined it.

"Damnit, Jojo, what's wrong?"

William's voice was quiet, gentle, but John still hesitated. In all their years as siblings, he had never asked William for advice, not like this. Trouble was, he did not really have anyone else to ask.

"Do...do you think we assume too much about ladies?"

Even John could hear the stupidity in his question, but there did not seem to be any other way to articulate it. *How could he begin?* How could he even think to explain the ridiculous situation he had managed to get himself in?

He looked up and saw William examining him closely, brow still furrowed. He looked as though he wished to ask a great number of questions, but after a close examination of the younger man, he sighed.

"Yes," William said. "Look at Charlotte. Everyone who saw her merely saw the surface level of who she was. They saw a chaperone."

John nodded. *That was, after all, what he had seen at first.*

"And though she performed that duty, she was so much more than a chaperone," continued William with a wistful smile. "It was only because I ignored society and all their gossip and took the time to know her, *really* know her, that I uncovered the jewel I now have as a wife."

John sighed. It was exactly as he had feared. His real affection for Miss Darby had blinded him to her feelings. If he had just stopped to think, to see her, *really see her*, he would have known she loved him. *Those damned letters!* Why had he not paid more attention to her, sought to see below the surface?

Rebecca Darby was his perfect woman. Last night had proved that, but instead of grasping her when he had the chance, he had lost her.

"I think," John croaked, "I have made a huge mistake."

There was no mistaking the curiosity on his brother's face. "Can you unmake it?"

John shook his head. "I...I do not know."

His stomach tightened painfully again.

"Bad stomach?"

Sighing, John knew it was time to admit the truth. "William, I'm in love."

REBECCA PLUMPED UP the cushion to the best of her ability, glanced at her father, and then continued to punch it into a more convenient shape.

"There you go, Father," she said quietly. "Is that more comfortable?"

Mr. Darby leaned back in his leather armchair, and a smile crept over his face as his back sank into the cushion.

"Much better, thank you, Rebecca," he said quietly, his eyes slightly shut. "Though I would be more comfortable if you were married, and to a good man!"

Rebecca sighed. *The same old conversation, the one they had been having for years now.*

She had been foolish to think she could escape it this evening, particularly after she had been visiting a friend the evening before.

At least, that was what she had told her father.

I should have returned to my bedchamber after supper. It would have been lonely, yes, but she would have avoided this age-old conversation.

She swallowed as she looked at the grey lines across her father's face, the way he flinched if a cushion was not adequately protecting his back. He was old. He had been old when she had been born, near fifty.

She should spend as much time with him as she could, she knew. *Who knew how much more time she would be given with him?* When he was gone, and the thought made her stomach twist, she would miss these evenings, these debates even if she loathed them now.

"I know you believe it is imperative I marry as soon as possible, Father," she said quietly, pulling a blanket over his knees, "but I am still only two and twenty years of age. There is plenty of time, I believe, for me to find a husband."

Her words did not calm the elderly gentleman. In fact, it appeared to have the opposite effect; the mention of her age, Rebecca knew, was always a sore subject for her father, who believed young ladies should be married before they reached their twentieth year.

His brow furrowed with concern, and his light blue eyes met hers. "Two and twenty, two and twenty! In my day, you would have a child, or maybe two or three, by that age!"

Rebecca nodded. "I know, Father, but this is not your day. It is my day."

How she could say that with such defiance, she was not sure. She was always respectful to her father, naturally, but there was a limit!

"In my day," continued her father, ignoring her, "ladies were married before—"

"—their twentieth year, yes, I know," said Rebecca as calmly as she could, moving a small table beside her father's chair and placing a glass of red wine upon it. "You have told me before, Father."

Mr. Darby's eyes narrowed as he watched his daughter sit down carefully on the sofa beside his chair and pick up her embroidery.

"And yet, you never listen," he said sadly.

Rebecca heaved a great sigh and remembered to smile as she said, "I do listen, Father, but as I said, that was then, and this is now. Things are different now."

"Now that's a true word," said the older man as he reached for his wine. "In my day, a lady would be ashamed to be unmarried at your age!"

Rebecca was forced to bite down the retort that sprang to her lips—*namely, that he had not married until he was forty, and it was most unfair to have such differing rules for the sexes!*

The words would not have gone down well, and as she picked up her needle to continue with the rose and ivy pattern she had started last week, she plastered a smile across her lips.

"I do not see what you have to be so cheerful about," muttered Mr. Darby.

Rebecca sighed. She knew it was difficult for her father. The world had changed, and he had not changed with it. Besides, any conversation with him was sure to spare her further thoughts of John.

Blast, she had been so good this evening at ignoring the thought of him.

"And there are no eligible gentleme—"

"Father, I am unmarried," Rebecca said, allowing her embroidery to fall into her lap. "Yes. But what do you expect me to do about it? A young lady cannot simply walk up to a gentleman she likes the look of and propose marriage, can she? You would not like me, your daughter, to act in such a wanton way, would you?"

Her heart twisted as she said these words. She hated being so direct with her father, who did mean well, but her pain was particularly acute after last night.

For that was precisely what she had done, had she not?

"No, of course not, that would be scandalous!" Mr. Darby looked uncomfortable at the very thought. "But...well, there must be ways for you to..."

Her father's voice trailed away. It was clear, Rebecca could see, that he was not entirely sure how the wiles of ladies worked. That they had worked on him thirty years ago did not exactly make him an expert.

"And you are old now, compared to the debutantes coming out at fifteen, sixteen," he continued plaintively.

Rebecca put her embroidery aside again. She could not allow this line of conversation to continue! Could he not see how she longed for a husband, for an establishment of her own—in short, for John?

"I will marry who I wish, Father, and I wish in this moment that you would stop pestering me about it!" she said with a little fire. "I am well aware of my age and the increasing numbers of young ladies entering society, but I can neither stop them nor propose to a gentleman. If you love me, you will leave this subject alone."

There was silence in the drawing room, save for the crackling of the fire.

"Rebecca," said her father eventually, his eyes wide. "I did not know you had it within you to be so direct."

Direct? Rebecca had never considered herself a direct woman. That was always something she had aspired to, but her chattering, nervous tongue had always meandered around a topic so long, most people had no idea what she was attempting to say.

There was a brash taste in her mouth, and only after a moment of introspection did she realize it was…anger.

Anger at her father? No, it was all directed at herself. She had done precisely what she had just told her father she could never do, and look how that had ended up?

John, the Lion of the Lennoxes, now knew her affection for him, that she had willingly ruined herself, given up her innocence to tempt him into matrimony.

If only he had not been so disappointed when he had seen her.

"I am sorry, Father," she said quietly. "I do not mean to be so direct. I do not know what has gotten into me."

When she looked up, however, Mr. Darby was not upset. Quite the opposite, he was grinning.

"It was like your mother was here, for a moment," he said gently.

"Mother? She was—well, quiet. Shy, retiring."

Her father nodded. "Yes, most of the time. But when the occasion demanded it, she was like a lioness when crossed. Your mother had fire within her, a fire I rarely saw, but when I did…"

His voice trailed away, and Rebecca saw a tear trickle down his cheek. Mr. Darby wiped his eyes.

"I think I will go to bed. I am most tired," he said quietly.

Rebecca's mouth was still open, and she wished to ask more about her mother, about the woman she could barely remember—but it clearly pained her father. In a way, it pained her, too.

"I will leave you by the fire," Mr. Darby said as he rose to his feet.

Rebecca nodded, unable to speak, and was left alone.

John. It was only now she was in solitude that she could really give him much more thought.

She had felt so brave, so bold when she had her mask on. When John did not know who she was. When the reveal was still far away, and she could indulge in being the person she had always wished to be.

Was that a part of her mother within her, starting to show itself? Was there a little more fire in her than she had ever known?

The Lyon's Den. There was something about that place, something she did not understand. It had given her confidence.

Whatever it was, Rebecca was determined to be that person more often. It was her true self. She knew it. She owed it to herself to be happy, even if John did not want her.

CHAPTER ELEVEN

I F HE WEREN'T careful, John was going to see his luncheon all over again in the opposite direction. His stomach squirmed, and he placed a hand over it in the hope it would calm down.

'Tis just nerves, John thought as he tried to force down the worries creeping up into his heart. All he had to do was stay calm. *How hard could it be?*

Rebecca Darby, in that mask, that gown. Rebecca Darby, out of them...

He had not understood himself, and he had certainly not understood her, but all that was behind him now. He had to leave it there, or he would not have the courage to do what he must do this evening.

It had been a challenge, even for him. The battlefield did not hold as much terror as the Lyon's Den, not after what he had experienced there. Not after what he had lost there.

But he had to come. Fool, though he was, he had harnessed all his self-control and battled his shyness to come here this evening, in preparation for—

"Ah, John Lennox."

The voice was scathing, if it was possible to be scathing in just four syllables.

EMILY E K MURDOCH

John turned to see Mrs. Dove-Lyon glaring. The proprietress of the Lyon's Den was not very happy to see him. But if he could not face down a woman and her disapproval, he did not deserve the hand of Miss Rebecca Darby.

"Good evening, Mrs. Dove-Lyon," John said, bowing low.

When he straightened up, he saw he had not entirely convinced her of his worthiness to return to her establishment, but at least she had not called for two of her ladies to remove him from the premises.

John swallowed. *This was not going to be an easy evening, he had known that, but if Mrs. Dove-Lyon could make it less difficult, that would be appreciated.*

"I am grateful for your help in this matter," he said quietly. They stood in the same room where he and Rebecca had...*well, there was a reason he could not look at the bed.* "Thank you, Mrs. Dove-Lyon."

She sniffed imperiously with quite the look of disdain. Even Lady Romeril, if she had ever deigned to know her, would have been impressed.

"Do not think I do any of this for you, young Lennox," she said stiffly. "Remember, you have not convinced me with words, but with guineas. I hope your words have more effect with the next lady to step into this room."

"So do I," said John fervently, but Mrs. Dove-Lyon was gone before he could say another word.

The door slammed behind her, and John was left in silence and solitude.

He coughed into the emptiness. *This was not a mistake; he was utterly sure of it.* He knew what he had to do—or at least, he knew what would be needed to win Rebecca's heart.

Though he had worried his heart's resolve would start to falter, the long waiting period here in this room calmed him. The more he waited, the surer of himself he was.

Of her. *Rebecca.*

Only now did he start to understand the fear and anticipation she must have felt when she had concocted her plan to seduce him. It was incredible she had managed it.

He had almost changed his mind many times throughout the day.

The door opened, and John turned to the two women walking in. One was dressed in what he recognized now as the uniform, more or less, of the Lyon's Den. She looked formidable, and the name Hermia hazed into his memory.

John's gaze shifted to her companion, blindfolded, and with her hands outstretched, and his heart twisted.

Rebecca.

Despite the blindfold, it was easy to see she was nervous. The gown she was wearing was of the latest fashion, not the artfully ripped and torn one she had on two nights before.

And yet, she was more beautiful, more alluring. John cleared his throat as though that would force down his intense attraction.

"There we are," said Hermia quietly in a reassuring voice. "Just a few minutes, and then you can leave—I promise you."

She gave John a stern look as she released her grip on Rebecca's shoulders, leaving her anchorless in the middle of the room.

John nodded. *It was all going to plan, at least, for now.* Who knew what was about to happen, now he had Rebecca before him?

Would his voice hold? Would he say what he wanted, what he must speak?

The door closed quietly. Hermia was gone, and there was silence in the room. In that instant, John's shyness overwhelmed him, and he stood mute, unable to move, unable to speak.

He swallowed, tasting fear in his throat. He had to say something! *Speak, man!*

But no words came to his aid. It was impossible to think about where to start. Where on earth could one begin?

It was Rebecca who broke the silence with a sigh. "I have risked much to be here, so this had better be important, John."

John stared in utter astonishment. *How in God's name…?*

"How did you know it was me?" He cringed at the petty tone in his voice. He was a gentleman, a marquess! He should not be cowed by a conversation with the woman he loved!

Rebecca shook her head. "Really? Think now, John. Who else would bring me here?"

Stepping forward, he removed her blindfold and fought the strong impulse to kiss her, there and then. She deserved better than that. She deserved to know why she was here and what he wanted from her.

Rebecca glared, and John took a few steps back.

"Look," he said hastily, knowing he had to get his words out quickly before his courage left him. "I made a huge mistake."

Rebecca nodded. "Yes, you did. You should not have agreed to marry me."

"No, that is not it at all," said John with a nervous smile. "I...I should not have waited for you to tame me. I shouldn't have waited for a gamble. I fell in love with you months ago. I should have done something about it. I should have proposed marriage to you. I should have told you how much I loved you."

THE WORDS WERE English, and yet they did not make sense. They couldn't. Not coming from John's mouth.

Rebecca swallowed and attempted to collect herself. *What was he saying? That he...that he loved her?*

"Look," John said into the silence, sighing heavily. "I am not too proud to say when I have made a mistake, and I have made a huge mistake."

How was it possible that his words still cut her so deeply? Mistakes, love, it was all too mangled together for her to discern y what he wanted. *Did he just want to insult her further? Say that he loved her, but that it was a mistake?*

Her concern must have been visible on her face, for John swiftly stepped forward.

"Please, do not misunderstand me. Miss Darby...Rebecca, I have never been one of sharing my true feelings. 'Tis easier to jest and quip with the ladies rather than share my...my heart."

There was real anguish in his features, and Rebecca found the protective walls she had built around her heart the last few days start to crumble. *He had said he loved her, hadn't he?*

"*I...Rebecca, I fell in love with you months ago. I should have done something about it. I should have proposed marriage to you. I should have told you how much I loved you.*"

But those were empty words, easy to say, easy to promise. Why had he not spoken them before?

Part of her wanted to reach out and touch him, feel the reassuring strength of his presence, but Rebecca knew she would never control herself if she did.

John had such a way about him. He was sure to convince her of anything if she got too close. Besides, she needed to understand before she allowed her heart to get away from her.

Was he...was he saying...?

"You say you should have said something before," she said hesitantly. John nodded. "Why did you not?"

"I told you, in this very room, that I w-was shy," said John quietly to the floor. "I spoke the truth. 'Tis most difficult when one is suddenly thrust into a titled family, to adhere to society's expectations. I can be quick with my tongue, but only when...when it does not matter. When I lost my heart to you."

Rebecca took a step toward him. It was impossible not to. Everything within her was drawn to him, the man she loved, the gentleman she had adored for so long.

She had risked so much to be with him, and now it appeared...well, if she was not mistaken, that he wished to be with her, too.

Was it all too good to be true?

"Most gentlemen do not bother to understand the woman before them," she said quietly. "Most gentlemen, when they are jesting, do not consider matters of the heart."

It was then that John looked up with a wry smile. "I did not realize my heart was in any danger until it was. From that moment, I have wanted to…wanted to say things I did not have the words for. Wanted to offer for you, Becca."

The longing in John's voice made her body warm all over, and he stepped forward. He was right before her now, only inches away. If she had the temerity to, she could have reached out and touched him.

"We made love on that bed, and you blush when I call you Becca?" John said teasingly.

She laughed shyly. "Well—well, yes, I do not know why."

"Becca, I want to marry you."

Rebecca gasped as John reached out and took her hand in his. *This was—this was…*

"*You.* The Miss Darby I met at the opera, *and* the Titania I met in the bedchamber," John said with a smile. "The one who commands me, the one who excites me. The woman I stole kisses from in the rain outside the opera house, and the woman who sat on my lap and drove me wild."

Rebecca laughed as John squeezed her hand.

"I wanted to marry you before, and I did not have the courage. You knew I needed to be tamed. Marry me, Becca."

The last sentence was more a plead than a request, and it took all of her self-control not to launch herself into his arms and allow him to kiss away all the pain of previous misunderstandings.

But first…

Rebecca took a deep breath. "You promised to marry me in this room not a few days ago. What…what makes this different? Are you going to keep this promise when we leave the Lyon's Den?"

She could not bear to think John might not keep his promise, but she had to be sure.

John nodded. "You are the Lyon Tamer, and I am merely the lion. I will happily spend the rest of my life showing you just how much I love you—and discovering more about you."

Rebecca stared into his eyes and saw the truth, giving her such happiness, she barely knew what to do with herself.

She was going to marry John. She would be the Marchioness of Gloucester, but more importantly, she would be Mrs. John Lennox. *John's wife.*

"In that case," she said, emotion spilling into each syllable, "I accept."

"Oh, Becca!" John rose to his feet and pulled her into his arms, kissing her furiously.

Rebecca responded just as passionately. This was her husband. She would never have to be alone or misunderstood again.

"Becca, I love you," murmured John as he broke the kiss and smiled. "And I cannot wait to be introduced to your father as your future husband, but—"

"Oh, lord," said Rebecca with a wry smile. "That is going to be an interesting conversation…"

"But before then," interrupted John, glancing at the bed behind him, "before we leave here…"

EPILOGUE

J OHN TOOK A deep breath in the cold, brisk air.

Well, after all his supposed cleverness, after thinking he was so witty, so impressive, this happy day had arrived, and really, he could claim no credit for it.

None at all.

It was all Rebecca. She had managed to seduce him, show him what he was missing, and given him—*finally*—the confidence to do something about his affection.

Love that had been waiting for the right time, he could see that now. Thank goodness she had been braver than him.

Now they would never have to be apart.

Time to go inside. They were all waiting for him.

"Where have you been?" Rebecca's bridal gown suited her perfectly, a smile on her face.

Their wedding day.

"I just took a moment outside for a breath of fresh air," said John, taking her by the hand. "You know, better than anyone, how easy it is to become overwhelmed."

His last sentence was spoken low, so only his bride could hear him.

The ceremony had been short. John could barely remember it

ALWAYS THE LYON TAMER

now.

And now, despite her shyness, the new Marchioness of Gloucester was welcoming her husband's friends and family to their home with just as much confidence as a woman born with a title.

"My daughter, yes, little Rebecca," came a voice.

John heard Becca sigh heavily. Her father was seated in a large armchair by the fireplace in the hall with a crowd of people around him. He looked rather pleased for the audience and was speaking in a loud, carrying voice.

"Now, I had assumed my little girl would not be married, being as she was over the age of one and twenty…"

John winced and glanced at his bride—but she seemed entirely unruffled. In fact, Becca laughed.

"He is not wrong," she said with a grin. "He did think that. He even told me so once. Come, let us leave him by the fire. It can do no harm for him to tell his stories as he sees fit."

He would never cease to be amazed by her.

"Remind me," John said quietly as they stepped across the hall and into the drawing room, in which some of their most important guests were milling, "to never underestimate you."

Becca laughed. "What, because I finally managed to convince you to marry me? It took me almost two years, John. I do not think I deserve praise for that!"

Despite her words, her smile was broad. There was something different about her. The Miss Darby he had first encountered at old Axwick's wedding was still there, of course. The same chatter, passion, and enthusiasm.

Yet, this creature was more refined. And he loved her!

"Charlotte…"

The sound of her name caught the attention of John's sister-in-law, for she turned from her conversation with the Duchess of Axwick and stepped lightly across the room.

"My ears are burning," she said matter-of-factly. "What have I done, or better still, what am I being accused of?"

John laughed. He had always liked Charlotte, even before she had married William.

"No such terrible thing, I assure you," said Becca reassuringly. "I was just saying that this wedding could simply not have happened in time without your help and support."

"Nay, you do not take enough credit—I assure you, John, that woman has more lists about her person at any one time than a tax collector!" Charlotte said with a sparkle in her eye. "I was hard-pressed to keep up with her!"

The two ladies giggled, and John found his heart, already full of the activities of the day, grow with a little more joy.

Family. That was what was important to the Lennoxes.

"You were the one who introduced me to—"

"Ah, well," said Charlotte impressively, waving a hand. "You spend years as a chaperone, and you start to know everyone in society."

Becca laughed and turned to John. "This woman really does know everyone. I do not know how she does it! When I asked for roses—"

"Yellow roses," interrupted Charlotte. "Yellow roses at this time of the year!"

"—Charlotte did it, of course," Becca continued.

"Gown, flowers, cake, all in time—it was merely child's play," said Charlotte. "And speaking of—no, William, get down!"

She rushed away, and John's gaze followed her—and met the sight of young little William about to topple over a vase.

"I always knew, you know."

John had not noticed his brother approach, now leaning on an armchair with a knowing smile.

"Known?" repeated Becca.

William nodded. "I always knew it was you, Miss Darby—or now,

I should say, Lady Lennox."

John saw the pleasure glow in her cheeks when addressed by her new married name, but he could not allow such pronouncements to go by unchecked.

"Always knew? How?"

His older brother shrugged. "You are so different when with Miss Darby—my apologies, it will take me a little while to acclimatize myself to your new title. Lady Lennox."

Becca glowed. "I, too, am finding it a challenge."

"I noticed it when we first went to the opera—nay, at Axwick's wedding," William corrected himself.

John grinned. "I am surprised you even noticed we were there, considering how obsessed you became with Lady Charlotte."

The gentle teasing prompted a nudge from William. "Well, can you blame me? Look at her!"

The newlyweds tilted their heads to look over at the Duchess of Mercia, who was seated on a sofa on the other side of the room, her young boy in her arms.

William sighed. "But I am serious, John. If you had just told me that you were thinking of Miss Darby, I could have helped you. Charlotte could have—"

"Don't you be thinking of offering your wife out as a chaperone, you brute!"

John laughed. The interloper to their conversation who had spoken so boldly to the Duke of Mercia was their youngest sister, Prudence.

"She has you bang to rings, William," he said easily as Becca giggled at the mock outrage on her new sister-in-law's face. "I know Charlotte has said goodbye to the chaperone life."

"Well, perhaps," admitted William. "But still, I stand by what I said. Your wife brings you alive. Any fool should have seen it."

"What you mean to say, though you are too polite to say it," said

Becca teasingly, "is that I have tamed him!"

The siblings and Becca laughed, and John wondered whether any other day would top this. Here he was, surrounded by the people who mattered the most to him in the world, laughing and jesting together.

His shyness had not mattered, not in the end.

Prudence had snorted in a most unladylike way at Becca's words. "Tamed him? John? My word, Rebecca, I do not envy you that task, and I would say Honora would agree. Have you seen her, John?"

Something twisted at his heart. Prudence may be the youngest of the four Lennoxes, but it was always Honora he worried about. *Especially after...*

"No," he said quietly. "Though I would not pay much attention to my memory at the moment—I can barely remember the church service, and that was only an hour ago!"

Becca squeezed his hand. "As long as you do not use that as an excuse to wiggle out of our marriage!"

Ignoring the crowd around him and the proximity of his sisters, John did what came naturally in that moment; he swept his beautiful wife into his arms and kissed her soundly on the lips.

"Oh, John!"

"I have no wish to see that!"

"Put that poor woman down!"

John was grinning as he broke the kiss, and so was Becca—though admittedly, her cheeks were hot.

"I will never forget about you, don't you worry," he said quietly, so only she could hear. "You tamed me a long time ago. I just did not know it."

"No, I am sure she is around here somewhere," said Prudence. "I will continue to search. Honora?"

In a swish of skirts, she was gone.

"I don't know, worrying about Honora," said William with a shake of his head. "We cannot simply continue to treat her like a—careful!"

The head of the Lennox family rushed away, arms outstretched, and as John looked over, he saw little Elizabeth, the youngest member of the family and William's toddling babe, had tipped over, bumped her little head, and was now screaming fit to burst.

John's brow furrowed with concern, but Becca put a placating hand on his arm.

"She is quite well, 'tis only a bump," she said calmingly. "I do love your family. I am so fortunate they have taken me into their hearts."

John's own swelled with pride. "How could they not? The Lennoxes may have gone through tough times, but we have always had each other, and now I have you. The perfect piece to complete the set."

Becca raised an eyebrow. "Or the last lioness to join the pride?"

It was all John could do not to melt right before her, but he had to regain some sort of dignity.

Thankfully, there was a small door behind them that led to a little passageway between the rooms. John pulled his new wife through it. The corridor felt unnaturally quiet after the uproar of the drawing room.

There was a look of concern on Becca's face. "Why are we—"

"I cannot wait to see you naked again," said John with a low growl. The pain of not being able to ravish her was starting to overwhelm him, and if he did not make love to her soon…

Becca smiled, and there was that spark of confidence which the Lyon's Den had given her. "You will never have long to wait every day of your life. But remember, I am the one in charge here."

"Lyon Tamer," breathed John as he crushed her lips beneath his.

About Emily E K Murdoch

If you love falling in love, then you've come to the right place.

I am a historian and writer and have a varied career to date: from examining medieval manuscripts to designing museum exhibitions, to working as a researcher for the BBC to working for the National Trust.

My books range from England 1050 to Texas 1848, and I can't wait for you to fall in love with my heroes and heroines!

Follow me on twitter and instagram @emilyekmurdoch, find me on facebook at facebook.com/theemilyekmurdoch, and read my blog at www.emilyekmurdoch.com.

Printed in Great Britain
by Amazon

21244148R00061